Whispers of Home

Pickleville Book One

April Kelley

Hard Rose Publishing

Contents

Whispers of Home

♥

Tragedy brought him home again. Can love convince him to stay?

Jaron McAllister has a son to raise. How can he do that when tragedy strikes, and the city he had once found welcoming, becomes more dangerous by the day? The best course of action is to go to go back home to the small town he'd once run away from. The last thing he expects to gain is the attention of a hot cowboy.

Travis Heath isn't looking for love. As the richest, most popular guy in his small town, he's had plenty of dates and one-night stands over the years and that's been just fine with him. When little Jaron McAllister comes back home, looking more gorgeous than a person has a right to, Travis is forced to rethink his views on commitment.

Jaron isn't looking for love, especially not with a man with commitment issues. Will Travis lose his best friends when they find out he's crushing hard on a man?

Whispers of Home is a MM Contemporary Romance in the Pickleville series. If you like down-on-their-luck single dads and bisexual cowboys with commitment issues, then you'll love this sensual romance novel.

Warning: Contains scenes of bullying and a violent hate crime.

This is a republished story that has been completely rewritten and re-edited. It also has new content and added chapters. It is the start of a nine-book series.

Prologue

♥

T he last day of senior year in Miss Larson's class looked exactly like the first day of senior year. The same kids sat at the same desks. Stonewashed jeans rolled at the ankles, and feathered hair marked every guy the same. The girls had bright, baggy T-shirts that covered high-waisted jeans. No one distinguished themselves from everyone else, including Jaron McAllister. Different wouldn't bode well. He had already proven himself quite different on the inside, and everyone knew it.

The anticipation at getting to the end of the year jumped around in his gut, creating butterflies as he counted down the last twenty minutes of high school. And apparently even his bladder didn't want him to sit there any longer.

The problem with going to the bathroom lay a few seats in front of him. Jackson Bartlett sat forward in his seat, flirting with Miranda Giles.

Miranda used to be his friend, but somewhere around seventh grade that changed. Jaron wasn't sure why, other than Brad Flynn forced Jaron out of the closet that year. Whatever. By the end of the day, neither one of them would ever have to see each other again. Well, they both lived in the same small town where everyone knew each other. They were bound to see one another from time to time. He planned on packing up and leaving town at some point after the graduation ceremony anyway.

Jaron raised his hand.

"Yes, Jaron." Miss Larson smiled as she met his gaze. She had a red ink pen in her left hand. As teachers went, she wasn't the old fuddy-duddy type. She had been a new teacher in their school at the beginning of the year. By the end, all the kids liked her because she gave them cool books to read and didn't yell. She wasn't that much older than Jaron. Maybe five years or so. All the straight guys liked her because she was pretty. She had auburn-colored hair that hung in soft curls around her face.

"Can I go to the bathroom?" God, Jaron had to pee so bad his lower abdomen hurt.

"Can I go to the bathroom?" Jackson mocked like a second-grader.

Everyone in the classroom laughed, except Jaron.

He tensed and glared at both Jackson and Miranda.

Jackson gave him the finger.

Miss Larson gave Jackson a look that made him lower his finger. When she turned her gaze onto Jaron, she smiled. "Go ahead, Jaron."

"Thank you," he said and made his way between the rows of desks. He had no choice but to pass by Jackson and Miranda because they sat in the aisle ahead of him.

"Fucking faggot."

Jaron was pretty sure Miranda sent that one his way.

"At least I'm not making my way through the entire basketball team, Miranda." Not that rumors told a true picture of events, but half-truths told part of the story. The half that held the truth had to do with Travis Heath. Everyone knew he made his way around the school, too. It seemed likely the two would come together at least once.

Sleeping with Travis wasn't why he threw that in her face. She wasn't a slut for sleeping with a bunch of guys. Or if she was a slut than Travis Heath was a giant one too. Jaron didn't think others should slap that label on anyone or judge someone else's choices.

No, the only reason he said anything was because she mentioned his sexuality as if it were a bad thing. Jaron was gay. So what? And he wanted her to understand that judging hurt, although his teaching method was childish.

Living anywhere else but in Pickleville would make his life so much easier.

The halls were almost empty. A girl stood at her locker, pulling out a book. Whatever book she read held her complete attention. Another girl walked ahead of him. She went through a door on the right into the girl's bathroom. The boys' bathrooms stood next to it.

Some of the lockers had numbers painted in green glitter with an athlete's name underneath. Pickleville was a small town, so the same kids who played football also played basketball. At the last pep assembly, the principal called the athletic kids well-rounded, but they didn't get scholarships to college because they were good enough to make the Pickleville teams.

The second Jaron pushed the bathroom door open and saw Brad Flynn standing at the sink washing his hands, Jaron wanted to turn and leave. He hesitated in the doorway when Brad sneered at him.

He almost left, but then he heard Travis Heath hum something and didn't want to look like a scared loser in front of the hottest guy in school, not that Travis even gave him one ounce of attention.

He shored up his courage and tried to ignore the way his heart rate picked up enough that he heard it in his brain.

The door swung shut behind him.

The stalls and urinals took up the left side of the room. A small school meant only two urinals and Jaron wasn't using the one beside Travis. No way would he give either one of the boy's ammunition. He headed for the farthest stall instead.

Neither boy said anything.

Travis didn't even look his way as he finished at the urinal.

Brad, on the other hand, watched him in the mirror.

Jaron could feel that gaze trail him like a stalker.

The sinks were on the opposite side, and Brad stood at the last one which was closer to the end stall. That was the one Jaron intended to go for because the wall was on one side and that made him feel less exposed.

Brad got to the stall before Jaron. He smirked as he held the stall door open. Jaron stopped, his body stiffening. "Go ahead."

Jaron shook his head and put his hands into his pockets.

"I'm not gonna hurt you." Brad made it seem as if Jaron was ridiculous for thinking otherwise.

Jaron would have left and just forgotten about using the bathroom until after he got home or used the one over by the gym. But Travis turned, giving him a smile when he crossed to the sinks.

Jaron smiled back.

He tried to relax, but he could still feel his shoulders up near his ears and knew he probably seemed like a scared nerd, which summed him up well.

Brad's smile fell the closer Jaron got, but didn't fully disappear until he straddled the line between inside the stall and out. The stall door slammed into him, the lock mechanism digging into his side, tearing his shirt and probably making him bleed, but he couldn't feel anything past the adrenaline.

Jaron tried to catch himself before falling into the stall divider, but his face landed against the edge. The impact sent him backward when he bounced off the stall divider. He landed on his ass with a cry.

Brad laughed. The sound echoed off the concrete walls.

Jaron shoved himself next to the outer wall and the front of the stall, pulling his legs up to his chest. He stiffened when Travis closed the distance in two long strides. He scowled as he met Jaron's gaze.

Jaron scrambled even closer to the front of the stall, shoving himself in the closest corner.

As soon as he did that Travis darted his gaze to Brad. Both boys had been friends for a long time, and it showed in the silent way they had a conversation.

"He had an accident." Brad smiled.

Travis reached a hand down to Jaron. He hesitated to take it, not wanting to trust it for the kind gesture it seemed. As soon as he did, they'd hurt him some more. Still, the beat down would prove worse if he didn't.

Jaron took it. Travis pulled him to his feet but let go of his hand immediately. "Is that true?"

Jaron nodded, not wanting to make waves on the last day of senior years.

Travis didn't look as if he believed it, but he took a step back. "Well, be more careful. You could hurt yourself."

Both boys turned to leave. Brad pulled a small bottle of liquor out of his jeans pocket. The bottle probably only held a couple of ounces. Brad held it out to Travis. "Took it from my dad after he passed out last night. Want a swig."

"Nah. I gotta help Leonard in the cow barn after school. Can't have alcohol on my breath. He'll know and tell my dad."

Brad shrugged and took a sip.

Jaron went over to the sink and tried to clean up as best as he could. His shirt had blood on the side. As soon as he saw the gash, it began to throb. Funny how getting a visual was the thing that started him on the trail of pain. "Shit."

Brian came barreling in a second later. "Gina told James that Brad Flynn was in here with you."

Jaron put his shirt down and turned on the faucet, washing his hands. "I'm fine."

Brian gave him the once over, assessing him. He put Jaron in the fine category, coming over to him and put a hand on his back. "You still thinking of leaving after the graduation ceremony?"

Jaron nodded. Physically, he was fine with a little cut that would heal in a couple of days. Mentally, he felt jumpy and ready to run as far as his legs could take him like a trapped rabbit. "Pickleville sucks." The little bathroom incident only proved that point.

Brian looked away, his hand disappearing. "We could get an apartment together. My dad would help us. You know he doesn't care that I'm gay. He wouldn't care if I had a boyfriend." At the last sentence, Brian averted his gaze.

"I just...I need out." Jaron turned away from the sink and headed out into the hallway with Brian beside him.

"I'll come out, too." Brian whispering so no one else could hear, told Jaron the real truth. No one wanted to get bullied, including Brian. Just because high school had finished, didn't mean that would change.

"It's not really about that." Or it wasn't all about that. "I just don't want to be here anymore." He wanted...freedom. He needed to see what was out there.

"It's not gonna be the grand adventure you think. And what if I need you. Did you ever think of that?" Brian's tone had turned from pleading to angry as if he were figuring out he couldn't hold Jaron down. If Brian had his way, he'd strap Jaron to the visitor's sign at the edge of town and keep him there forever.

Jaron didn't respond. If he said anything back, he might get sucked into Brian's needs, and Jaron couldn't let that happen. He was none of the things Brian needed. Brian hadn't realized that yet. "Maybe you're supposed to come with me. Did *you* ever think of *that*?"

"My dad has a job for me after college. It's all set up." Brian's dad owned an accounting firm. His dad fully expected Brian to take over when the time came, and Brian wanted the same thing. Jaron wished his own mom gave a shit half as much as Brian's dad did. He was a great father who would move heaven and earth for his son, including sending him to the best university possible and providing him with a job after.

Something bigger than Pickleville waited for Jaron. He just had to go out and find it. If he stayed, he would end up an angry, resentful old man. Worse of all, it would be Brian he resented most. And Brian was his only friend.

When he made his way outside, he found his mother waiting for him in the long line of parents. He waved goodbye to Brian and hopped in the car. "I could have walked."

"I have to work in thirty minutes." Nothing about that explanation made sense as to whether he walked or not.

Jaron sighed and nodded even as he clicked his seatbelt into place.

"Gotta work all weekend. I'm staying with Nancy in between." Nancy lived right across the street from the factory. Mom always stayed there when they had mandatory overtime. "You can have the car. Just drop me off."

Right. So she only came so she could ditch him. It wasn't a *last day of senior year, so I won't make you walk home* type of thing.

"Okay."

"You want grocery money?"

"Nope."

"You sure?"

"I'm sure, Mom." He was always on his own, so what difference did it make? "Last day was today."

Mom made a noncommittal response as she pulled out onto the road. "You'll have to tell me about your day on Monday."

"By then it won't matter." Jaron looked out of the window as she drove down Main Street.

Chapter One

♥

Jaron slathered peanut butter on a cracker and slid it across the table to Bobby. Bobby took it with a smile and contemplated a way to shove the whole thing into his mouth. Jaron gave him the dad look. "Small bites."

"Okay, Papa." Bobby's blue eyes had a way of sparkling with mischief even when trouble didn't intend to stalk him. His blond hair hung across part of his forehead, giving him an impish quality. He bit his cracker and kicked his legs to a rhythm only he heard.

Tracy came into the room with a T-shirt that had a panda on the front and pajama pants with clouds all over them. She had lost a bit of weight in the last couple of months, which had always been a sign that she'd started using again.

Jaron's gaze went to the inside of her arms, searching for track marks, but he couldn't see anything. He sighed in relief and turned away. "You look tired."

She smirked at him as she poured herself a cup of coffee. "Thanks. I got in late last night."

She dug around in her pocket, holding a wad of cash in her hand. She laid it on the table in front of Jaron, and then sat next to Bobby. "Momma got some dough." She ruffled Bobby's hair.

Bobby gave her an annoyed look, which made her laugh.

It would have made Jaron laugh too, but he couldn't take his eyes off the money next to the peanut butter jar.

"Where did you get it?"

Tracy smiled at him. "Does it matter? At least I'm contributing. Now you can stop complaining."

Jaron shook his head and slid the money across the table to her. "It does matter. I thought you finished with that."

Tracy rolled her eyes and slid the money across the table again. "I'm not using meth."

"Another cracker, Papa."

Jaron gave Bobby a smile. He slathered peanut butter on a cracker and slid it over to him.

"I gotta work in a few minutes. Are you gonna stay sober enough to take care of Bobby?"

When Tracy stood, the chair scraped across the linoleum. "How many times do I have to tell you, Jaron?"

Jaron narrowed his eyes. "You have a lot of trust to build back. Throwing d-r-u-g money at me isn't exactly winning you points." He spelled the word *drug* because he didn't want Bobby exposed to that kind of thing. His mother being an addict was enough of a problem.

Bobby stiffened, and his shoulders came up to his ears. He placed his half-eaten cracker on the table.

Jaron smiled, softening his facial features as much as possible. Arguing in front of him had already done the damage, though. Jaron could see the wariness in his eyes.

When Tracy sighed and reached out to him, her palm held open for him to take. Jaron shook his head but placed his hand in hers. She smiled and met his gaze. "I know. I'm trying this time, Jaron."

After five years of her saying that same thing and then using again, believing her didn't come easy. They'd been down that road before and Jaron needed to turn off it for Bobby's sake. Even selling drugs, she'd only stay sober for a few months before she shot up all the profits. "I don't want your dealer boyfriend coming to me because you owe him money. I won't pay it like I did the last time."

"I'm not gonna do that this time. Vince takes care of me." A sparkle entered her eyes, and she wiggled her eyebrows.

"'Vince'?" It took him a minute to figure out who she meant. Tracy had a lot of friends. She had one of those personalities that made her a fun person to hang out with, even when she got high all the time. Sometimes she brought her friends around, but she never distinguished them as boyfriends or guys she fucked. And Jaron didn't care enough to pay attention. He only cared if she brought lowlife creeps around Bobby.

"Motorcycle and bandanna."

Jaron lifted his eyebrows. "He's in a gang, Tracy. Selling drugs with him is a big mistake. His gang is not one you should mess with."

Tracy let his hand go and shrugged. "He's making sure I stay clean. Doesn't let me shoot any of the drugs I sell." She lifted her chin. "That's how I know I'll stay sober."

Her thinking was completely backward. "Just keep him away from Bobby."

"I know. We're not that into each other yet." Tracy always said the same thing about every guy she dated. The only difference was the business arrangement she had with Vince. That might complicate things in ways she hadn't thought of yet.

"Selling is a dangerous business."

"I know what I'm doing."

"Famous last words." Jaron passed the jar of peanut butter and sleeve of crackers across the table before he stood. He kissed Bobby on the head. "I gotta go, snuggle bear."

"Gotta go to work." Bobby's bright blue eyes flashed at him.

"That's right. I'll bring you back some fries. Be good for Mommy." Jaron walked around Bobby's chair and kissed Tracy on top of her blonde head. "Do me a favor and stay home today."

"I wasn't gonna go out until after you came home."

Jaron nodded and put on his shoes. He heard Tracy and Bobby talking, but he couldn't hear what they said.

The diner sat on the corner of Fifth and Water Street. The building fit the corner, designed to catch the eye with its strange shape and large windows at the front. The booths had red vinyl and white tabletops. At some point in the past, the wait staff comprised of females in dresses with aprons covering them, but that had given way to jeans and a T-shirt with the diner's logo on the front, and gender stopped mattering. It had been a diner since the day someone had decided to build it, and it would remain one into the distant future.

The diner had a life of its own. People moved around and through it. It seemed content with remaining stuck in time with its long, white counter and red stools. Businesspeople had turned to first responders and police officers when the station had gone in on the next block over in the 1960s. A few tourists and regulars made up the rest of the patrons.

Jaron knew the history behind the building because some city official marked the place as a historic site and placed a green plaque next to the front door sometime shortly after the city had finished building the new station. Jaron knew the words by heart because every time he started his shift he went through the front door instead of using the back like the other cook. The sign drew his eye, and his mind latched on until he had the thing memorized.

Jaron patted Jody's shoulder. He had no idea what Jody did for a living, but she always ordered breakfast burritos and ate them between typing on a laptop.

"Hey there, sweet." Jody could multitask so well. She could make extra money giving lessons.

Jaron smiled. "Hey. You look like you're working hard."

Jody smirked. She pulled her dark hair away from her face and didn't bother putting on make-up that morning, not that she needed it. She had a pretty complexion without it. "Always have a deadline. Always."

Jaron moved around her, waving to his best friend, Andrew and his partner, Mike. The two of them ate there twice a week. "How's Bobby, vato?"

"Fine. Fine. Watching too much television this summer."

"Did you get him signed up for school yet?" Andrew had dark circles under his eyes that spoke of the harshness of his job.

Jaron never asked about Andrew's detective work, and he watched the news once a week at best. Even he'd noticed the spike in murders.

Andrew hung onto a cup of coffee with both hands and didn't let go even when Jaron slid up next to his booth. Andrew moved over and let Jaron sit next to him.

Jaron had about fifteen minutes before his shift started. He always came early, wanting to socialize a bit before work.

"Not yet. Not sure about putting him in a city school."

Andrew raised one dark eyebrow, which made him look like a badass. Just one. Jaron wished he could do that. It would make him seem a little mysterious. Every emotion he felt lay all over his face, so no mystery. And he pretty much said whatever he thought the exact moment the thought occurred.

"You and Tracy gonna put him through private school?" The way Andrew looked at him, he doubted their ability to afford that, and he wasn't wrong.

Jaron snorted out a chuckle. "On a cook's salary? Not hardly."

There went that eyebrow again. "Then what you gonna do?"

Jaron shrugged. "Not sure yet." He'd been thinking of Bobby's wellbeing more and more. He and Tracy lived in a poor neighborhood. They couldn't afford to live in the suburbs where schools held less violence and a better curriculum.

"Fall's coming soon." Mike spoke around a mouth full of eggs and toast.

"I know."

"How's Tracy?" Andrew probably already knew the answer to that question. He didn't suck at his job. He might investigate homicides, but he had friends in other departments and resources he could use.

Jaron leaned in and whispered in his ear. "She says she's clean, but she handed me a wad of cash right before I left for work." He might feel weird telling a cop about Tracy selling drugs but he didn't know if he cared if Tracy got caught. Maybe that would finally wake her up. Tough love and all that.

"Need me to go over there and check on them?"

Jaron shook his head. "I think she's staying sober for a while this time." He worried about the guy she got the drugs from, though. Jaron would give it time, and if the guy turned even a little bit dangerous, he would tell Andrew.

"I just hope she stays that way." Andrew let go of his mug and slid it over to Jaron.

Jaron hoped so too but the only time she had ever stayed sober for any significant period was when she was pregnant with Bobby. That had been when they'd first met. Two weeks after delivering she'd gone out and gotten high.

He smiled and took a sip of Andrew's coffee. "So, how's your mom?" Nothing better than changing the subject. Tracy's drug addiction saddened him, and he had a whole eight-hour shift to get through. Better to do that with a happy attitude.

"Worried and tells me every day." Despite Andrew's words, he had a smile on his face.

Jaron lay his head on Andrew's shoulder. "Can't say I blame her. You work too much."

"It's not the amount I work, vato."

The other detective nodded. "Amen to that."

Connie, who owned the diner and worked as a waitress most days, gave him a look.

Jaron nodded and moved from the booth. "I'll talk to you later."

"Call me if you need me to go get Bobby. Mami would love spending time with him."

Jaron nodded. "Thanks."

Andrew would make a great father and partner in life. He didn't see that in himself, though. Jaron wasn't sure why. "I mean it, vato."

"Okay. I'll call home soon. See what's what. I'll let you know how that goes. Deal?"

"Deal."

Jaron leaned in and kissed Andrew on the cheek. He had a five o'clock shadow just starting. It poked at Jaron's lips. Jaron ran the back of his fingers over it. "You need time off, I think."

"Tell that to the criminals."

"I've been trying, but you cops keep them out of the diner." The diner wasn't in the part of town where most of the criminals hung out, not with the police station so close. It lay in a little bubble of peace most of the time — a sanctuary where Jaron had friends and people who understood him, sometimes better than he understood himself.

Andrew grinned. "Go make these hungry people lunch and leave me in peace, cabrón."

Jaron turned and headed to the opening in the counter. He tapped his ass, silently telling Andrew to kiss it.

Chapter Two

♥

Jaron's apron had hamburger and fry grease on the front of it. He probably smelled like what he cooked, but his senses had gotten used to it over the six years he worked there. He took off his apron and hung it up on the hook by the small opening that separated the kitchen from the rest of the diner.

He searched for Connie through the opening, finding her talking to some regulars. The diner had slowed down until patrons took up two booths. One booth held a couple of emergency responders. They had on blue uniforms with a radio strapped to one shoulder.

He yelled out to her. "Taking my break. I'm using the phone in your office."

Connie waved a hand, letting him know she heard.

He made his way to the door of the office, which was just off the kitchen on the left. Jaron left the door open and made his way over to the phone, dialed his home number, and waited. And waited. The longer he stood there listening to the ringing, the more his stomach ached, and a certain kind of familiar dread took over his body.

After so much ringing, he hung up.

He took off his hair net, threw it in the trash can on his way through the kitchen, and headed out into the main diner.

Connie stood behind the counter, pouring a cup of coffee to someone Jaron had never seen before.

He walked over to her. "I gotta go home."

Connie nodded. "I'll call Eddie if I need him."

"I'll come back if everything is fine."

Connie met his gaze, holding the half-full pot of coffee suspended in her hand. "Yeah, we both know it's not gonna be. Just make sure that sweet boy of yours is okay. Bring him to work with you tomorrow if you gotta."

Jaron smiled. "Thanks, Con. Just gonna call Andrew real quick, and then head out of the back door."

"Go. Go."

Jaron turned back into the kitchen, and then to Connie's office. He dialed Andrew's cell number and waited. It took him less than two rings to answer and when he did, Jaron didn't waste time getting right down to the problem. "Tracy didn't answer when I called."

"I'm on my way."

"Thanks."

Neither wasted any more time on conversation, which Jaron appreciated. He wanted to get to Bobby as soon as possible.

The poor kid didn't need to be alone. Hell, he didn't need to have a drug addict for a mother, but Tracy hadn't ever been anything else.

He headed out of the back door, stepping onto the sidewalk just as Andrew pulled up. Jaron got in, pulling the seatbelt around. The click it made as the belt hit home was the only sound either of them made.

Andrew pulled out onto the road again, flowing with the rest of the traffic.

Jaron wiped his palms down his jean-covered thighs and thought about what to do if he found Tracy high again. "Maybe she took him to the park or something."

"Maybe." Even though Andrew agreed, Jaron knew it wasn't likely.

"If she's...I'm done. I can't do this again." He whispered the words more to himself than Andrew. "I have to think about Bobby. I've let him see too much already."

"The city is filled with drugs. For an addict, it's hard to get away from it." Andrew turned down a side street that would avoid most of the traffic. "I see it every day. Hell, the only thing our narc detectives do is help contain the problem. At the end of the day, getting the addicts sober and arresting the dealers is too much. We're spread too thin."

Jaron watched Andrew, studying him. They'd been friends almost since the first day Jaron started working at the diner, and Jaron hadn't seen him quite so stressed before. "Is everything okay?"

Andrew nodded. "Working on a hard case. Seems like one right after the other."

"Maybe you need a break."

Andrew darted his gaze to Jaron before turning it back to the road again. "Maybe you do too."

Jaron shrugged. "Maybe." He'd been thinking that very same thing more and more. The longer Tracy's addiction affected Bobby and the older he got, the more Jaron thought that raising his son in the city would prove detrimental to Bobby's development. "I just want to do what's best for Bobby." The more he thought about it, and the more time that passed with Tracy fighting addiction and losing, the more Jaron realized that what was best for Bobby probably wasn't further exposure to her illness. "She's sick."

"Yes."

"I can't afford rehab." And she needed that type of help.

"It's not all on you."

"We're all each other has."

"Oh, really." Andrew gave him a look. "I'm chopped liver now. And Mami would be upset to hear you say that, cabrón."

"You're right. I'm sorry. I'm all she has." Jaron patted Andrew's arm.

Andrew nodded and turned down another street. The closer they got to Bobby the more a feeling of dread settled into the pit of his stomach.

Jaron and Tracy had shared an apartment since the day he agreed to father her unborn child. They had wanted to create as normal an environment for their son as possible. Both had grown up with single parents. For them, normal meant two parents living in the same household. It was what they had seen on television growing up.

He learned quickly that normal was overrated and meant different things for everyone.

Their apartment had been a big house at one point, but someone had renovated it and made four apartments inside. The shell of its past held up on the outside, though. The tenants accessed their apartments from the front, even the ones on the floor above. Thankfully, Jaron didn't have to climb stairs to get to his apartment. The downstairs apartment had seemed like a good idea when they'd moved in but seeing their door halfway open made him rethink that decision.

Jaron's stomach twisted in knots as he reached for the door handle. Andrew grabbed his arm. When Jaron met his gaze, he shook his head and reached for the communication device all cops seemed to have. "Ten sixty-two. Requesting backup." He rattled off Jaron's address before reaching under his sports jacket and pulled out a gun.

Jaron's hands shook as he opened the door. Andrew held on to him tighter but he pulled his arm free. "Bobby."

Andrew sighed, but he let Jaron go. "Stay behind me."

He wouldn't make any promises, but he waited for Andrew to make his way to the open front door before following him.

The door opened into the living room. An old couch Jaron had picked up at the thrift store sat on the left side of the room against the wall. The coffee table didn't match anything else in the room, including the couch, but it served its purpose well. A scale and small baggies were scattered across the table. Some lay on the floor, barely visible as they blended into the carpet. A gallon-sized bag filled with white powdery crystals sat next to the scale.

Jaron would have gotten instantly pissed except for the big man sitting on the couch with his eyes like a fish. A red stain covered his upper chest on the left side.

Tracy lay face down. He only saw the upper half of her body. She faced the wall and had a gun in her right hand. The carpet near her chest area was darkened and looked wet with blood.

Andrew said something to him, getting in his face, but he couldn't hear anything past his own intake of air. Andrew cupped the back of his neck and forced Jaron to meet his gaze. Jaron exhaled.

Time slowed down.

"Bobby." Jaron's heart beat loud as he breathed out that word. He stepped away from Andrew when his chest hurt, and the panic set it. "Bobby!"

Jaron turned and ran down the hallway, screaming Bobby's name.

He heard sirens in the distance and Bobby calling for him from his bedroom. Jaron noted the blanket-covered lump in the center of his bed. He ran over and threw back the covers, revealing Bobby's healthy little body.

Jaron couldn't keep the tears at bay when he picked Bobby up and held him. Bobby wrapped himself around Jaron. His little face tucked into Jaron's neck. "The mean man hurt Mommy."

Jaron carried Bobby out of the room but then stopped in the middle of the hallway, meeting Andrew's gaze when he came around the corner.

"Is he all right?"

"I think so." Jaron ran a hand down Bobby's back. "Did anyone hurt you, snuggle bear?"

"The mean man tried, but Mommy wouldn't let him." Bobby never lifted his head from Jaron's shoulder.

Andrew gave Jaron a look. "You'll need to take him outside. Stay there until I come back out."

Jaron nodded. "Shut your eyes and don't open them until I tell you. Can you do that?"

"Cause Mommy's hurt?"

Jaron let the tears flow again. He thought about lying, but Bobby saw the whole thing. Lying would do more harm, not less because it would confuse him. His voice shook when he answered. "Yeah, snuggle bear."

Jaron did what Andrew told him. He kept a hand over Bobby's head as he carried him through the living room.

Chapter Three

B y the time Andrew came out of the house, Bobby had fallen asleep in Jaron's arms. Jaron sat on the neighbor's lawn on the other side of the yellow police tape. If the neighbors minded, they didn't say. They didn't come out of their house, but looked through the front window, sliding the curtains back. They didn't offer Jaron and Bobby help or even something to drink, not that Jaron would have been able to hold anything in his stomach anyway. In the three years Jaron had lived in the house, he'd never talked to them. The neighborhood wasn't the type that someone could go up to a house and knock.

Cops were everywhere. In and out of the open doorway as if they lived there. He expected paramedics with body bags to roll up the sidewalk, but they weren't ready for that step yet.

When Andrew finally did step out, he wasn't alone. A cop, who dressed a lot like Andrew, in a suit, stood beside him, and the two spoke. Jaron couldn't hear what they were saying past the buzz of voices. They weren't trying to keep the conversation private, though. That much was clear in the way Andrew pointed at Jaron.

Both men crossed the yard, heading in his direction, but Andrew stopped halfway there, leaning against a tree as if waiting for something.

The other detective pulled a notepad and a pen from his pocket as he made his way over. The detective knelt in front of him, smiling at a sleeping Bobby, who looked peaceful despite the trauma he'd been through in the last few hours. His smile disappeared when he met Jaron's gaze again. "Detective Martinez tells me you live here with the deceased female."

Oh God, calling Tracy that drove the nice layer of numbness away until Jaron's emotions were raw again. A lump formed at the base of his throat. He tried to swallow it down, but that didn't work so he spoke around it as best he could. "She was alive when I left her."

"And what time was that?"

"Somewhere around ten o'clock this morning. I had the lunch shift at work. Should still be there." God, if Jaron wouldn't have called home than Bobby would have been alone for a lot longer.

Jaron pulled Bobby closer, putting his hand on Bobby's chest, feeling the air move in and out.

"Why'd you leave work early?"

"Tracy. She...she's an addict. Hasn't used in like two months and this is usually the time she starts back up again. So I called home to make sure she wasn't getting high around Bobby."

"When you called did you speak to anyone?"

"No one answered."

"What did you do after that?"

"Called Andrew."

"Why call Detective Martinez?"

"I work at the diner on the corner of Fifth and Water. Taking the bus would take too long. So I called Andrew for a ride."

"Did you expect trouble? Is that why you called him?"

"Andrew and I are close friends. He has my back. Always." He thought about the first question. "Tracy...she can be reckless."

Not anymore. Tracy's recklessness had caught up with her. She couldn't *be* anything anymore.

"In what way?"

"She trusts easily. That guy on the couch. His name's Vince. I saw him in passing once when he dropped Tracy off last week. He's part of that motorcycle gang that deals meth in this part of town. A bad guy." Vince was nothing anymore. Snuffed out like a candle. Not even a trickle of smoke. "This morning Tracy called him her boyfriend."

The cop wrote down what Jaron had said. "And how did that make you feel? Her having a boyfriend?"

Jaron shook his head and rolled his eyes. "I told her I didn't want Bobby around someone like him."

"You weren't jealous?"

He knew that's where the cop planned on taking his questioning. He had to cover all the bases and make sure Jaron hadn't gone in there in a jealous rage. Jaron could see by the detective's expression he didn't actually believe Jaron had anything to do with it. "Tracy and I were best friends."

"You the kid's father?"

"In every way that counts." He could see the confusion in the detective's eyes. He sighed before explaining his situation. "I met Tracy when she was five months pregnant. Tracy and I hit it off right away. Bobby's bio dad was some john of hers. We decided to raise Bobby together. Every kid deserves a dad, right?" Jaron's own dad left before he could remember the guy. As far as Jaron was concerned, his father provided sperm, nothing more.

"So platonic."

Jaron nodded. "Tracy's not exactly my type."

The detective wrote a few things down, putting his notepad and pen back under the flap of his jacket. "I might have more questions for you, so stay available."

"Andrew will know where I'm at."

The detective nodded and stood. He turned and closed the distance to Andrew. "He's all yours."

Andrew nodded, not taking his eyes off Jaron. He closed the distance between them and squatted down much the same way the other detective had. Andrew looked at Bobby, brushing hair off his forehead. "How are you guys holding up?"

Jaron shrugged.

"So they're not going to let you stay inside. How about you come home with me? Let Mami take care of you and Bobby."

"Thank you." Jaron wouldn't have been able to stay in their apartment anyway. "You don't have to stay and investigate or whatever?"

"Not my case. I'm way too close to the situation. And I'm as much a witness as you."

Jaron smirked. "You mean I'm not a suspect?"

"Nah. I'll tell you what we think happened in the car."

"Can I pack us some clothes and stuff?"

"I'll go in and do it for you." Andrew stood and bent down, holding out his arms to take Bobby so Jaron could stand. As soon as Jaron let go, Bobby came awake. His little body jerked right before screaming for Jaron. Andrew whispered reassuring words, but nothing he said calmed the panic.

Jaron came to his feet and took Bobby back. "Shh, Papa's got you. Papa's here."

Bobby quieted immediately. He shook even as he wrapped his arms around Jaron's neck and his legs around his waist, holding on as if his life depended on it. Given what Bobby had witnessed, he probably thought it did.

Jaron met Andrew's gaze. An entire conversation happened between them with just one look because they were both thinking the same thing. Kids proved time and again that they were a resilient bunch, but Bobby would suffer before the storm calmed. "Papa's not going anywhere. Ever."

"Mommy didn't wake up."

Oh God. Jaron shut his eyes as the emotions washed over him. "I know, baby."

"You'll wake up?"

"Always. I promise a thousand times."

Andrew cleared his throat. "I'll go pack that bag."

The seatbelt laws required Bobby to sit in the back, but none of the cops cared that Jaron sat in the front passenger's seat with Bobby on his lap. Bobby was still wrapped around him, not moving even when Jaron pulled the belt around them both, and Andrew got the car moving.

Bobby slowly relaxed, and his breathing evened out again. For a kid who fought naps on a regular basis, stress seemed to send him over the edge needed for a peaceful nap to happen. Jaron would take the boy who fought him with everything he had, if it meant Bobby didn't have to go through watching his mother die again.

"He asleep?"

Jaron rubbed circles on Bobby's back. "Yeah."

"You want to hear what we think happened?"

Jaron swallowed down the lump in his throat that never quite went away. "Yes."

"You sure? It's not a pretty story."

"Just tell me." He'd rather have it ripped off like a bandage. As hard as it was to hear, it wouldn't get any easier.

"So based on the evidence, it looks like the male victim shot first. We're testing for gun residue to make sure. Based on what Bobby said, it appeared the male shot Tracy. She had a wound in her abdominal region. As fatal as it was, it didn't kill her right away. She fought with him and somehow got the gun away. Shot him. We think he might have been high. He's a big guy, so it's unlikely she overpowered him otherwise."

"Tracy protected Bobby. She wasn't the greatest mother, but she wouldn't have let him get hurt. Maybe her maternal instinct made her stronger."

Andrew shrugged. "Can't rule it out. My mom has a protective instinct to rival anything."

Jaron shut his eyes and let the hum of the engine lull him for a bit. "I think...I think I'm gonna move back home." He didn't even know he intended to say that aloud until the words were out, floating around his brain, burrowing in until the thought became a good idea.

"Home? As in crappy farm town where it 'sucked so much, you don't even know Andrew'."

Jaron chuckled through the tears. "I don't sound like that."

"Yes, you do, vato."

Jaron opened his eyes again. "I think raising Bobby here would be a mistake. He needs stability and as much as it scares me to move back, I don't have the money to go anywhere else. I'll need my mother's help."

He wasn't worried about the gossipmongers in Pickleville so much as the bullying in the school system. He'd had two main bullies, which didn't sound like a lot with an entire school full of children but two was enough. Especially when everyone else had done nothing to help the situation. Not most of the other students or most of the teachers.

But even that was better than the violence and lack of academic structure of the schools in the city.

"He has stability with you. You know that."

Jaron took a deep breath in and then let it out slowly, calming himself from the inside out. "I let Bobby see too much. Drugs were all over the living room. Bobby had to have seen them, and he's heard us talking about the stuff Tracy got up to. Once he gets in school, the kids around here will try to sell it to him. He'll get as hooked as his mother. I can't do that to him."

"You blaming yourself for Tracy?"

"No." Jaron's thoughts were in a jumble and he was in panic mode. He had to be if he contemplated moving back to Pickleville. Articulating took more time than he cared for, but Andrew didn't seem to mind the silences in between the explanations. "I think...I'll never get out of that neighborhood. Doesn't matter how many shifts I take at the diner."

"Keep going. It helps to talk."

"That damn neighborhood, with the drugs and guns, sucks people in until they do things they ain't proud of, and I can't afford that. Bobby can't afford that."

Andrew nodded. "I've made arrests in that part of the city plenty of times. You're right about it being bad news. But you ain't like those others."

"Not yet, but what happens when the rest of Vince's gang finds out they lost him and one of their sellers. We both know they'll kill me if I don't agree to sell for them. I'm not a good enough liar to be a criminal. I'd be in jail inside of six months. Then where would Bobby be. Foster care."

"I'll shut down that gang's operation. You have my word on that." Andrew's jaw ticced out a rhythm that spoke of his conviction. "When are you thinking of leaving?"

"As soon as possible. I don't have a lot of money in savings, but I have enough for bus tickets and a couple of months helping my mom with bills and food." His mother would help him. He knew she would, even with the radio silence he'd given her over the last seven years. Parenthood had a way of making him see things from a different perspective, so he understood that working all the time didn't necessarily mean she didn't care about him.

Chapter Four

♥

Jaron felt Bobby's little fingers wrapped around two of his. In Jaron's other hand, he held a large duffle bag. He'd used the bag when he left Pickleville. The irony of that didn't escape him.

The bus wheezed, popped, and jerked as it rolled to life on its tires. As it moved past them, Jaron focused on the restaurant across the road. The restaurant had large windows in the front with the words *Bella's Restaurant*. Underneath that were the words *Pickleville, Michigan* as if the restaurant itself held pride in where it stood.

His mother held a mug, probably full of coffee. She held her thin shoulders forward which made her spine curve. Seven years had made her fragile in a way Jaron hadn't remembered her ever being. She stared into her mug as if it held some truth she longed to find.

Seeing her again through the window, made him feel as if he stood in the back of a movie theater. He watched as if it weren't real life. His life was that mug she held.

If she turned him away, he'd call Brian. If he refused, Jaron had enough savings to get them a place to live for about a month. Then he'd have to hope he'd find a job quickly.

When he had left all those years ago, he had been a stupid kid wanting to fit in somewhere. Everyone, including his mother, had known he didn't fit in Pickleville. Maybe he still didn't but he had to hope for Bobby's sake.

Jaron looked down when Bobby squeezed his fingers. He met Bobby's gaze and smiled despite the desperation pounding through his heart. He needed so much for the town where he grew up to magically turn into a safe haven for Bobby, even though it hadn't been for him.

God, please.

A door behind him opened, changing Jaron's focus, making him stiffen. Everything about Pickleville made him tense up as if he were that eighteen-year-old kid dealing with bullies and gossipmongers.

The building had housed a hobby shop called the *Hobbyist's Dream* but had turned into an Asian market at some point. The shop next to it had been a movie rental place when he'd left, but that had transformed into a florist. On the bus ride through town, he saw that someone had put a fast food place by the highway. The hair salon over that way was an ice cream shop.

Maybe things *had* changed.

"I'm thirsty." Bobby spoke around the thumb in his mouth. Jaron thought Bobby had dropped the habit a few months ago, but it reared up again, probably caused by the stress.

"Me too. Let's go." Jaron stepped off the curb and onto the street, gripping Bobby's hand just a little tighter, pausing for a car, and then continuing until he came within inches of his mother, the glass providing the only barrier.

She met his gaze, showing more emotion in those few seconds than he had ever seen during his entire childhood.

He was the first to look away, but that was only to make his way inside. When he entered the restaurant, the familiar smell of diner food hung in the air, calming some of his nerves.

A man greeted him, pulling out an adult menu as well as a children's one along with a packet of crayons. "I don't need a menu." Jaron nodded his head in his mom's direction. "Meeting her here."

"Right." The man smiled but handed him the children's menu and crayons. "In case he wants to color."

"Thank you." Jaron took the offer and closed the distance between himself and his mother.

Mom had never been a big talker and nothing about that changed. Not even when he sat across from her tucked into the seat next to the window.

Jaron wasn't a big talker either when he was nervous, so it came as no surprise when Bobby was the only one making noise.

His mom watched him, her gaze darting to Bobby, who tried to hide behind Jaron's arm.

Every few seconds Bobby whispered, "thirsty."

His mom smiled at Bobby and waved the waitress over.

"What do you want to drink?"

Jaron knew the woman because she had been in his grade. They graduated the same year. She hadn't changed that much other than carrying a few more pounds than she had back in high school, but they looked good on her. Her name was Beth Calhoun, and he remembered her as a happy, smiling girl who made friends easily. That one quality reminded him of Tracy, which brought tears to his eyes.

"Two lemonades please," Jaron told her.

She gave him a look as if his sadness concerned her, but she didn't know how to approach the subject.

He kept the topic on food. "Two hamburgers and fries too."

"Sure." She smiled and turned to the counter.

The silence took over again. Jaron wrung his hands together and tried to avoid his mother's gaze.

Bobby laid his head on Jaron's shoulder even as he played with the paper menu and handed Jaron the box of crayons to open. Four different colored sticks sat inside. Bobby chose the blue one and moved off Jaron as he colored a picture of a hippo.

The waitress dropped off their drinks, which gave Jaron something to do as he pulled the paper off the straws. Bobby's drink came in a small white plastic cup with a lid so he wouldn't spill it.

In all that time he couldn't bring himself to meet Mom's gaze.

To his surprise, Mom was the one to break the silence.

"I thought you were dead. Did you know that?" Her hands shook even though she still held onto her coffee cup. Steam curled in front of her face.

"No. I didn't." He didn't know what else to say. An apology was inadequate, not that he thought she needed one. Explaining why he had left wouldn't help her get over the hurt.

The waitress placed the food in front of him and Bobby, but he felt sick to his stomach. He picked up a fry and dipped it into ketchup anyway.

Jaron gave Bobby a smile.

His mom cleared her throat. "I'd like to know where you've been."

"The city. Like I said."

"And you had a bad time there?"

Jaron met her gaze. He put his hamburger down. "No, Mom. It wasn't bad at all. I had friends and a job I liked."

She frowned as if wanting to ask a bunch of questions but didn't know where to start. "What's his name?"

"Bobby."

She smiled when Bobby looked up from his food. "Hello, Bobby. Where'd you get such pretty blue eyes, huh?"

Bobby moved into Jaron again, trying to hide behind his arm.

Jaron smiled. "From his mother." He wasn't ready to talk about Tracy and all that had happened. Maybe he would, but he understood Mom wanted to fill in the huge gaps his absence left. "How about I tell you about her later." She opened her mouth to speak, but Jaron held up his hand. "It's not a nice story. And...I can't right now. Okay?"

Mom nodded. "You both must be tired."

Jaron nodded and took a bite of his sandwich.

His room was exactly the way he had left it. His Metallica poster still hung on the back of the door. The lead singer's long hair and the white lettering on his black shirt the only relief against the black walls he had loved. The red comforter hadn't been moved or made in seven years. Dust covered everything.

He had forgotten his juvenile need to be mad at the world.

The white letters above his bed read *Scream*. He had forgotten that part of himself too, but it came back in stark relief. All at once, he realized the hurt he felt had followed him around for years after he moved away.

When had the anger dissipated?

Probably sometime after leaving town all those years ago. And then Bobby came, and he had no time for anything else. Tracy had been immature enough for both of them.

He had changed. Life happened, dragging him through the mud, forcing him to either lift his head or drown. He swam through the mud pies. Each one he got through left him better than the total of the contents in his childhood bedroom.

Bobby hung onto him as if he were about ready to fall into the deep. They both held each other up, although Bobby would probably never know just how much.

Jaron looked down at the small angelic face.

"The spare bedroom can be his if he wants." His mom came into the room. She held out fresh sheets. He took them from her.

"Thanks. He probably won't sleep there." Jaron set the sheets down on the cleanest surface he saw. The floor. Why had she never dusted? It was as if she froze him in time.

"He'll have toys and such."

He nodded, turned to the bed and began to strip it of the soiled blankets and sheets. It was difficult with a five-year-old strapped too him like a second skin. "Okay buddy, want to help me here?"

"I guess." Bobby pulled the thumb out of his mouth and pulled the sheet all without letting go of Jaron.

"Bobby, would you like to help me make cookies?" His mom asked, smiling, and holding out her hand.

He shook his head and burrowed closer to Jaron.

"How about I go with you and watch you help?" Jaron asked.

Bobby nodded, and they all left the bedroom.

"You'll have to explain to me what brought you home finally."

"I know. I will. Just give me time. Please."

"I gave you seven years, Jaron McAllister. I think that's long enough."

"The mother of my child was murdered a few days ago. I'm a single parent raising a son who saw the whole thing."

"I didn't realize."

"Of course not." Jaron didn't know if he was ready to entertain whatever hurt feeling she had from him leaving. He wasn't even sure he was ready to admit that he caused that hurt.

She led them into the kitchen. Nothing in the room had changed at all. The coffee pot sat on the same part of the counter. Even the small beehive sugar bowl was exactly where it had been when he left. After living with the chaos that was Tracy, who hadn't put anything back in the same spot, he realized for the first time just how anal his mother was.

He chuckled even as he sat at the table.

Mom gave him a strange look.

He waved her off. "Tracy was messy." Something about those three words, let his emotions loose. He let out a sob before covering his face with his hands, not wanting his mom to see him cry.

Bobby's little arms came around him.

Jaron pulled him into his lap, and they hung onto each other.

"Crying doesn't make you weak, Jaron." There hadn't ever been a moment where he needed his mother more, and she seemed to know what he needed to hear. "Maybe if I would have shown more emotion around you, you would have felt differently about leaving."

Jaron met her gaze. She leaned against the counter, gripping the edge. "Maybe."

"We have a lot to talk about, you and I, but it can wait until you're ready." She owed him nothing and yet she let him upend her life.

"Thank you for taking us in, Mom."

She nodded and turned to Bobby. "We need eggs for cookies. Would you like to help me get them?"

Chapter Five

♥

Of all the things he thought he would do his first couple of weeks back home, lying around his mother's living room watching cartoons wasn't one of them. He needed to get out and get a job, but the thought of facing other people beyond Bobby and his mother tightened his chest.

So yeah, maybe he had a little bit of depression setting in, and he couldn't afford that particular illness. Not that depression cared what he could or couldn't afford. It didn't care about anything but settling into his body, shutting everything down so the monster could breathe.

And he fully admitted, at least to himself that he was scared to walk out of his mother's front door.

Jaron sighed and turned his head to look at Bobby, who snuggled into his side. Bobby had a cut up apple in a bowl next to him. He had his hand inside, lying over the bowl's lip, not taking an apple slice out, but holding one in his hand. The cat chasing the mouse held Bobby's complete attention.

Jaron smiled even as he kissed the top of Bobby's head. He stood and walked around the couch. "I'll be in the kitchen, snuggle bear."

He'd make a list of needed grocery supplies while he talked to Andrew.

"'k, Papa."

"I'm calling Andrew. You want to talk to him?"

Bobby scrambled off the couch, upending the bowl of apples until two slices escaped.

Jaron walked around the couch again, picking up the apple slices in one hand and putting the bowl on the coffee table with the other. He followed Bobby into the kitchen, where the phone hung on the wall. Before picking up the phone receiver, he threw away the apple slices and washed his hands. Jaron dialed and then handed the phone to Bobby. "Remember to ask for Andrew."

Trying to teach Bobby good telephone manners was an effort of trial and error. Andrew had been their guinea pig before, so he was used to it.

Bobby waited, listening to the ringing. "Andrew?"

Jaron rolled his eyes and shook his head.

"Grandma Gloria gives me cookies just like Grandma Louisa does." Bobby nodded as if Andrew could see him. When his eyes darted to Jaron, he knew Andrew said something about him. "Papa hugs me a lot...yeah." Again with the head nodding. "Okay...love you too."

Bobby handed the phone to Jaron and went back to his cartoons.

Jaron smiled as he put the phone to his ear. "Hey."

Andrew chuckled. "It's a good thing he's so damn cute."

"I had that very same thought."

"I'm sure."

Jaron pulled a notepad and pen from the drawer and opened the refrigerator. "How's it going around there?"

"Same thing, different day. Only difference is you're not at the diner." And Tracy isn't alive. That knowledge hung between them. "How are you?"

"I need a job. My savings won't last forever." He needed to leave the house more than once every two weeks. "Other than that, I'm fine."

"Have you met with any of your old friends?"

"You mean the one I had. No. And he hasn't called. Maybe he's waiting for me." Maybe he didn't realize Jaron made it back home. His hermit status didn't exactly give anything away, small town notwithstanding.

Andrew sighed. "Best just to get settled there. The sooner you do that, the better it will be for Bobby."

"You're right. I know. That's why I'm making a list to go to the grocery store." He wrote down the basics. Milk, eggs, and bread. He added cereal and cookies. He had it on good authority Grandma Gloria ran out of the cookies Bobby loved so much.

"The grocery store, Jaron. What does that have to do with anything?"

Jaron smiled. "The grocery store has a community board. It's the only place in town that will have job listings."

"No one uses the newspaper?"

"Nope. Not around here. At least they didn't when I left, and of all the things that have changed, I seriously doubt that's one of them."

"Small town thing?"

"More like a farmer's thing. Farmers post things for sale and when they need a farm hand. I think it's just easier for them to write a note and tack it on a board than to contact the newspaper or work a computer."

"Old school."

"Yep." Everything was old school around there, and no one cared about technology taking over the damn world.

Most residences in Pickleville had fields to harvest. Not everyone farmed but a good enough portion did that everyone else catered to that particular profession. Those who didn't farm usually worked in the next town over at the factory. His mother was one of them.

Jaron would rather work in Pickleville. He didn't have a car. Pickleville had a lot of land so traveling to and from work might prove difficult enough without him going to the next town over.

And he always had Bobby to think about. He wanted to be as close to him as possible all the time, even if Bobby was in school, which would have to happen soon.

"Tell Louisa I said hi."

"If you don't call her soon, she'll have a fit."

Jaron smiled. "I'll do that then. Take care of yourself, Detective."

"Maybe that small town of yours isn't so bad, huh, vato."

Jaron chuckled. "I'll let you know." He'd have to leave the house to find out just how Pickleville would treat him the second time around.

Jaron stuffed the grocery list into his front pocket and locked the front door behind him before putting his keys in with the list. He took Bobby's hand, and they walked together. Main Street wasn't very far away, and Jaron needed the exercise.

"Grandma's at work." Bobby swung their hands between them.

His mom had always worked nights at the factory before. Sometime in the last few years, she changed to the day shift. Despite Jaron not wanting to talk about the past few years and Mom needing to know, having her home every evening made for a pleasant time together. Whenever Tracy came up, his mom let Jaron steer the conversation away. Because she didn't push the issue, Jaron relaxed a little at a time every day.

"Yes."

"Will you go to work too?"

Oh no. The line of questioning wasn't good. So far, neither of them had left the other's sight. They both needed to know nothing bad would happen the way it did to Tracy. No matter how irrational the fear, it still lived inside them. But Jaron was an adult. They'd both have obligations that would separate them for hours out of every weekday.

Despite Bobby's age, even he understood that to some extent.

"Well, if I don't go to work, then I can't buy us what we need."

Bobby looked up at him. His face scrunched as he thought about that. "Like toys."

Jaron chuckled. "Yeah."

"Like a bike?"

"Yep. Exactly like a bicycle." Jaron turned right, heading into town. Main Street lay one street over, but Trenton Street had a sidewalk where part of Main didn't. He didn't want to walk Bobby down the side of the road when a safer route lay a block over.

Well, Pickleville didn't call the space between one road and another blocks. Everyone in Pickleville measured the same space in terms of miles. Two-tenths of a mile. A quarter mile. A half. That sort of thing. Jaron had gotten used to thinking of distance in terms of blocks. It would take a bit to go back to the small-town way.

"Can I go with you to work?"

"I don't know. You'll have to go to school."

Bobby shook his head. "No."

"Other kids are there. You could play with them."

"I don't want too."

"Why not?"

Bobby's shoulders came up to his ears. "I like just you, Papa."

"But you like Grandma too, right?" When Bobby shrugged, he decided to let it go. He wouldn't get anywhere by pushing, and he didn't leave Bobby with strangers anyway. Everyone in town was a stranger except for Mom.

Jaron turned right again. At the second house on the left, a young teenager came out of the front door. He had a guitar in his left hand and a pissed-off expression. His flannel shirt and cowboy boots made him look out of place in that part of town where all the houses sat close together. The guy belonged on a farm somewhere.

Yelling came from inside the house. The teenager winced and hung his head.

"Are you okay? Do you need help?" Jaron couldn't leave the kid to flounder or deal with whatever went on inside.

"'m good. Thanks." He walked past him down the road in the opposite direction.

"Do you need a safe place?" Jaron stopped and turned, watching as he walked away.

"Yeah, just have to call. And I ain't going back to that house."

"Yeah, I wouldn't either if I were you."

A door opened to the house across the street to the one the kid came out of and a little old lady waved. The teenager went right over to her. "I live over on Territorial Street. House number three sixty-five. If you ever need anything."

He nodded and smiled before he went inside. Jaron waited until he heard the lock fall into place before he turned back and kept walking.

"Mommy yelled a lot."

Jaron cleared his throat and forced himself to talk about it the way Bobby needed. "I bet that scared you."

Instead of saying whether it did or not, Bobby kept the conversation on task. "You don't yell."

"Not very often."

"You wouldn't yell at me."

"Did Mommy yell at you?"

Bobby shook her head. "At the bad man. He called me a bad word. She didn't like him doing that."

Jaron wanted to kill that fucker all over again. Tracy might have been a lot of things, but she protected their son with her own life. After all the arguments over her drug use and the disagreements, he wished she were there, so he could tell her how proud she made him. He smiled. "Mommy was so brave."

"We need to be as brave as Mommy, huh?"

"Yeah. We do." Tracy wouldn't want Jaron getting depressed.

She would love that he mourned her loss. She'd laugh her ass off and say that everyone should miss her. *I'm way too much fun, Jaron McAllister. You're no fun at all. That's why we balance each other out.*

How many times had she said that? Dozens. What Jaron viewed as irresponsible, Tracy had viewed as fun.

Maybe she was right. Maybe he took life too seriously.

Chapter Six

♥

It had been a long time since he'd been in the grocery store, and in all that time, nothing had changed. Not the board right inside the front door with business cards and written notes all over it, and not the gossipy cashiers who worked behind the counter.

Jaron grabbed a cart and swung Bobby up and into the seat. Bobby chuckled as Jaron made an airplane noise before settling him inside. He latched the cloth seat buckle that hung from the back of the seat. It probably wouldn't do anything to protect Bobby much, but it couldn't hurt either.

Jaron ignored the curious cashiers and dug the list out of his pocket. The whole time his hands shook, and he felt as if he were in high school all over again.

He had to remove his keys to get it all the way out, but he managed, putting his keys back. He handed the list to Bobby. "Okay, what does it say we need?"

Bobby blinked at him before he ran his finger over the word *Milk*. "Cookies."

Jaron raised his eyebrows with a grin and then leaned in enough to point to the first word. "Milk."

"Milk," Bobby repeated.

"Yep. To the milk aisle, Jeeves." Jaron made a show of pushing him farther into the store, making Bobby laugh. He put one arm up, holding Bobby in place when he turned the corner faster than expected.

One cashier walked over to the other one and leaned in, whispering something to him.

Jaron didn't know what they said, but they looked in his direction.

He had known the grocery store was the hub of all the gossip. Not even the restaurant rivaled it, although he had a feeling whatever gossip the mongers spilled around town started at the restaurant the day he arrived.

God, he'd almost forgotten how small towns worked. In the city, the gossip never really touched him at all. He had made connections so deep he considered them family, even though they didn't share any blood connections. Or he made no connection at all. Hardly anyone was just his friend. No one who cared would ever gossip about him. They'd tell it to him straight, having a conversation. Andrew was especially like that. Pickleville was different. Things were slower, and with that slowness came boredom. His presence had broken up the monotony for those bored few who had seen him in the restaurant, and those who would listen to the embellished story about them that day.

His presence in the grocery store would fuel the gossip fires for a while. People would get used to him and stop caring what he did, and during the entire process, Jaron would know not one of them truly cared. And that was okay because he hoped it would change for a select few. If it didn't, he'd find a different spot to call home.

"Leanne Shembarger's daughter is pregnant. Poor girl is only fifteen years old. You ask me, she should give it up for adoption." At least he wasn't the only one at the shit end of the gossip.

Jaron rolled his eyes at the two women standing in front of the coolers on the right side of the store. He smirked at them. "Excuse me."

One of them moved over, paying them little mind. "I heard it was Travis Heath who got her pregnant."

Okay, he might not want to pay attention, but he did when he heard Travis' name because he had been such a player back in high school.

The other woman waved away that comment. She had blonde hair and teased it until it resembled a light-yellow hive of bees. It didn't move at her animated gesture. "I don't believe that. He hardly leaves his farm since his father passed away. And he's never messed with an underaged girl."

Jaron grabbed a carton of milk and moved past them, refusing to listen anymore. He didn't like it when people made him gossip fodder, so he wouldn't do it to Travis Heath.

"What's next on the list, Jeeves?"

"I'm a snuggle bear. Not a Jeeves." The way Bobby said Jeeves was cute because he put an *a* at the end.

Jaron chuckled. "I forgot." Jaron leaned in and pointed to the next word. "Eggs."

Bobby repeated it, running his finger across it as if memorizing the sound each letter represented. The eggs were in the cooler next to the milk, so Jaron grabbed a dozen quickly.

"Next?" Jaron repeated the same process. "Bread."

"Bread."

They went down the bread aisle, and Jaron grabbed a loaf. The bread and cookies were across from each other, so Jaron pointed to the next word. "That says cookies."

Bobby's eyes lit up. "I want the little man cookies." Bobby pointed to the packages with elves on them.

"The fudge ones?"

Bobby nodded. Jaron grabbed them off the shelf and placed them in the cart.

"Good choice," someone spoke from behind Jaron. The voice was deep enough the guy could have said just about anything, and it would have sounded good.

Gossip about him and he shall appear. Travis Heath stood in front of the crackers, searching the shelves.

He'd gotten hotter since high school. And taller.

Jaron came to the guy's shoulders. Or probably did, anyway. It was hard to tell from down the aisle. What hair Jaron could see poking from under his cowboy hat, looked darker than Jaron remembered.

"I haven't seen you two in town before. Are you new to Pickleville?" He had a kind smile, but those eyes held a sparkle of mischief that told Jaron he better steer clear. If he didn't, he may find himself falling into Travis' charm.

"Something like that."

"You here to stay?" Travis said casually while looking over the crackers in the aisle. "Damn it. Why is it she needs the most obscure friggin' cracker on the planet," he said under his breath.

Jaron raised his eyebrows. "Which cracker?"

"Wheat thins or something like that."

Jaron spotted what Travis needed. "What flavor?"

"I have no idea."

"Well, they have two different flavors to choose from."

"Where?" he asked, his eyes scanning the shelf.

Jaron picked up a box and held it out. When Travis took it from him, their gazes met. "Thanks."

"No problem." Jaron cleared his throat and looked away.

Travis took his cell phone out of his jean's pocket and dialed. Before he even started talking, Jaron took off down another aisle and away from temptation.

"Papa, we should get the sandwich cookies too," Bobby complained.

"Next time." Jaron pointed to the next thing on the list. "To the vegetables, snuggle bear."

Bobby grinned and ran his finger over the word, whispering it to himself.

They didn't encounter Travis in the store again. It wasn't until they'd checked out and headed for home that Jaron saw him sitting in a fancy black truck. He had the driver's window rolled down and rested his tanned arm on the frame.

"Hey."

Yes, Jaron saw him. Yes, he pretended he didn't know Travis spoke to get his attention.

God, Jaron didn't even know why he ignored him other than the attraction was definitely one-sided and then there was the part where Travis didn't seem to recognize him. That left a minor blow to Jaron's ego, not that he hadn't expected it.

"Hey." Okay, ignoring him the second time was plain rude.

Jaron raised two fingers but didn't bother turning around. As it was, his hands were full of Bobby and groceries. He wasn't about to let go of either one of those things just to acknowledge Travis.

Travis pulled the black truck into a parking spot in front of the hardware store, which happened to be a store ahead of them. Travis leaned toward the open window. "Would you like a ride somewhere?"

"No. Thanks anyway." Jaron didn't stop. He walked faster until Bobby protested the speed.

"You sure?"

"Very." How many times had Jaron carried groceries and had a hold of Bobby's hand as they made their way home? Hundreds. And it usually took two buses too. Walking a couple of miles was easy compared to that.

And he didn't know Travis. Not really. They hadn't been friends in high school and, while Travis hadn't bullied him, his friends had. If he learned anything from growing up in Pickleville it was not to trust easily.

"I'm Travis."

Jaron stopped walking long enough to meet Travis' gaze. He rolled his eyes and shook his head. Why did he expect the richest, hottest guy in town to remember the little queer who'd gotten bullied every day since seventh grade?

Whatever.

Jaron started walking again. "Am I walking too fast, snuggle bear?"

Bobby shook his head and stuffed his thumb into his mouth. His brow wrinkled as if something bothered him.

"What's wrong?"

"Is that man going to hurt you?" Bobby lisped when he spoke around his thumb.

Jaron stopped and bent down. He made the best mean face he could. "You see this face."

Bobby nodded and smiled, his tongue poking out around the bottom of his thumb when he did.

"You think he'll bother us if I make this face?"

Bobby giggled, but the smile died when he looked at something over Jaron's shoulder.

"I'm suddenly regretting my decision to get out of the truck." Travis' voice startled him.

There wasn't a way to hide his reaction. He dropped the groceries, the milk tipping over onto its side, as he put a hand to his chest and sucked in air.

Travis chuckled and picked up his groceries. "Let me help."

Jaron stood. "Fine, I guess." When Bobby leaned into Jaron, he picked him up. If Jaron let Bobby walk beside him, he would plaster himself against Jaron, making walking awkward and Jaron had created enough awkward situations for himself around Travis already. They'd only exchanged a few words. "Thanks."

"It's my pleasure." They walked in silence for a couple of minutes, Jaron very much aware of Travis' presence beside him. Jaron's suspicion about their height difference was correct. Jaron came up to Travis' shoulder. His bigness didn't stop there, though. He had the farm boy thing down to a science with his wide shoulders and long legs. His tight jeans and snug t-shirt left little to the imagination, and still, Jaron wanted a picture of the guy naked.

Travis cleared his throat. "Couldn't help but notice you never gave me your name."

Jaron smiled. God, the guy was charming without trying. "Very observant of you."

Travis grinned. "Guess I'm just good that way."

"I guess so." Jaron rubbed circles on Bobby's back.

"Who's your little friend there?"

"My son, Bobby."

Travis reached over and tugged a lock of Bobby's hair gently. Bobby turned his head away. "How old are you, Bobby?"

Bobby held out a hand and all five of his fingers without facing Travis.

"Five. Wow, you're almost as old as me." Travis winked at Jaron when their gazes met.

Of course, Jaron blushed. He had one of those faces that showed everything he felt at the exact moment he felt it. He hoped Travis wouldn't interpret the blush correctly and figure out Jaron's attraction to him. He didn't feel like getting his ass kicked. Bobby certainly didn't need to see that, not after Tracy.

Bobby turned back and eyed Travis with a level of suspicion he hadn't had before Tracy's death. Maybe his caution was healthy after everything that had happened, but it still broke Jaron's heart that Bobby had to grow up a little faster in that one area.

Bobby took his thumb out of his mouth. "You're old like Papa."

Travis' eyes widened, and he let out a surprised chuckle. "Is that right? What do you think, Dad?"

Jaron chuckled. "I think you calling me Dad is weird."

"If I had your name, I'd call you by that."

There went that heat climbing into his cheeks again. "It's Jaron."

"So how long are you in town, Jaron?"

"A while."

After that, the questions stopped, and a companionable silence fell between them.

It wasn't until they stood in front of Jaron's house that Travis spoke again. "I just figured out why you look so familiar. You're Jaron McAllister."

"Yes."

Jaron set Bobby on his feet and dug for his keys. He unlocked the door and let Bobby inside. "I'll take those. Thanks for carrying them." Jaron smiled as he took the bag of groceries from Travis.

Travis pulled a cell phone from his jeans pocket. "Do you have a cell phone?" When Jaron nodded, Travis asked, "Can you text?" Jaron nodded again. Jaron didn't prefer using it, though. So he never carried the thing around with him.

"Let me get your number," he said stepping just inside the door.

"Why would you want it?"

Travis fiddled with his phone. "We can catch up."

"Catch up on what, exactly?"

"I get what you're not saying, okay. I was never your friend in school, but I would like to be now."

"Why?"

"Why do I have to have a reason to be your friend?" Travis' forehead got a cute wrinkled look between his eyes. The irritation in his voice gave Jaron pause, though.

"Forget it. Just get out of the way so I can close the door." Jaron made a shooing motion with his fingers.

Travis just stared at Jaron as if he'd lost his mind.

"Take no for an answer." Spoiled rich kids needed to learn they couldn't have everything.

Travis sighed and put his phone back into his pocket. "Fine."

Well, okay then. Travis could take no for an answer. That was an important thing to know about a person who lived in the same town. It paid to know who the creeps were.

Jaron rattled his phone number.

Travis turned, pulling his phone out again. "Tell me again."

Jaron repeated it before going inside.

It didn't even take Travis five minutes to send him a text. *Just wanted u 2 have my #*

Thanks

Can I ask u a ? Without u going off the rails.

Off the rails? I guess.

I thought u were gay in high school.

Did u?

R u?

Yes.

Bobby?

I had a good friend who got pregnant. She didn't know who the father was and I was there through most of the process. She put my name on the birth certificate.

O

What about u? Wife? Kids?

No and no. Love kids though.

Jaron smiled. *I think if someone doesn't like kids they are a little weird. Rumor has it u got some high school chick preggos.*

Lol. Nope. Just a rumor. Want 2 do something some time? Go out?

Don't know if that's a great idea.

Why not?

Idk. How did he say he had too much baggage? Plus, the attraction was there. No doubt about it. It was awkward to have a friendship with someone he felt that attracted too, when the other guy didn't feel it. Right?

Hell, he didn't know.

It's just hanging out.

Idk.

Why?

Aren't you afraid my gay will rub off?

Nope. Already halfway there anyway.

Wait. What! Did Travis just tell him he was bisexual?

Jaron sat at the kitchen table and stared at that last text.

Huh, he never saw that coming.

Jaron decided to change the subject. D*o you know anyone hiring?*

So you're gonna play it like that? Fine. My mom is looking for a housekeeper. That's about it. U need a job?

Yes. Very badly. Think she would hire me?

U want to b my mom's housekeeper?

Can't b picky right now. I got a kid to feed. Plus, Jaron could see himself liking a job like that. The solitude alone would fit his personality.

Right. Call my mom then. Her name is Beverly. She's in the book. Tell her I told you to call.

Thanks.

Any time. Got to drive. Ttyl.

U don't drive and text? lol.

Nope. And I don't fuck high school children. Just for the record.

Chapter Seven

T ravis didn't remember the drive home and wasn't aware of how he even got there until he pulled up outside the main house. Jaron had hypnotized him. He sat in his truck for the longest time.

Had he just told Jaron about his bisexuality?

He hadn't told anyone except for his dad. Dad hadn't told anyone except for his mom, although Travis only suspected that. He'd never asked her if she knew. The old man hadn't cared, so Travis hadn't made a big deal of it. He had sexual attractions to both men and women, leaning more toward women for some reason unknown to even him. It was what it was, so Travis hadn't thought about it that much.

Dad dying meant the farm had become Travis' responsibility. He didn't have time to date. That fact didn't change because he saw someone who interested him.

But God, something about Jaron knocked him for a loop. Never in his life had he experienced anything like that. More than attraction, although that was there too. So much more he didn't know what to do with it.

Greg came out of the bunkhouse and went into the horse barn. He looked as if someone had eaten the last of his favorite cereal, and Travis needed to find out why.

Travis put his truck keys in the center console before getting out. He headed into the barn and found Greg scratching Trick's big nose, whispering secrets to the horse.

"He's a good listener, but he doesn't talk back." Travis leaned against the other end of Trick's stall door. "Is listening all you want?"

Greg shook his head.

Travis couldn't begin to understand the things Greg had been through in his life. His parents loved him and each other. Although he didn't remember getting spanked, he remembered a few times when he'd deserved punishment. He might not have anything useful to say, but it didn't hurt to let Greg know someone had his back regardless of the current issue.

"I went to get my guitar today. It's the last thing I needed from home. Mom and Dad were fighting again and I had to call Leonard to come pick me up before meeting him at the feed store."

"I wish you would have called me. I was in town getting something for Mom. I would have brought you home."

Greg shrugged. "It's fine."

"That's not your home anymore, anyway. Hasn't been since the day you got to this farm. Your family is right here. You need me to send you inside the house to Mom to prove it?"

Greg smiled. "Nope." He cocked his head, looking thoughtful. "Did Bev bake recently? I'd go in for cookies or cake."

Travis chuckled. "You'll have to go in and see."

Greg nodded. His smile died. "I want to hate them. I should, right? I mean they put each other and me through hell."

"Whatever you feel for them is just fine. There's no wrong way to be." How many times had his dad said that last statement? It fit a lot of different situations. Hell, it even fit his feelings toward Jaron. Maybe he needed to take his own advice.

"Yeah, I guess you're right. I just...the guitar was the last thing, ya know. I don't have to go back to that house. It took two years to go back just to get the guitar. I don't know how I feel about that right now."

"I guess there's good and bad with that, huh?"

Greg nodded. "Yeah."

Greg came away from the stall. Travis slung an arm over his shoulders when he did, walking him out of the barn. Greg tried to walk toward the bunkhouse, but Travis held on. "Where are you going? If we have any chance for cookies, you're the one that's gotta talk Mom into making them. She won't do it for me. I'm not cute enough anymore. But you, you still have a baby face."

Greg chuckled. "So I'm like your puppy now. Using me to get what you want."

"You're the one who brought up cookies." Travis pulled the kid closer, hugging him as they walked into the house.

"I disagree that I have a baby face, for the record."

"You're young still. Twelve years old now, right?" Travis grinned as he led Greg around the side of the house to the back. Going in through the kitchen would get him yelled at less.

"Very funny. I'm eighteen. An adult." Greg gave him a narrow-eyed stare.

Travis chuckled as he pulled the back door open. "Well, don't let that adult thing scare you. You're still a kid to us. Our little fella."

Greg pulled out of his hold and made a face, making him laugh even harder. "No. Just...no."

"If you've been in the barn, take off your shoes." Beverly sat at the kitchen table with a book and a cup full of coffee beside her.

"Yes, ma'am." They both spoke at the same time.

Travis had his boots off first. He walked over to the sink and washed his hands. After he dried off, he made his way over to his mom and kissed her on the cheek. Travis sat at the table next to her.

She smiled and then waved Greg over, tapping her cheek in a silent bid for a kiss, which Greg gave her right before sitting down on her other side.

Beverly looked from one to the other. "Why do I get the feeling you two are up to something?"

"Because we are." Travis grinned and pointed to Greg. "He wants cookies. And I might have found you a housekeeper."

Beverly patted Greg's hand and smiled at him before turning her gaze onto Travis. "Did you get my crackers?"

Oh, shit. "I forgot to bring them in."

Beverly pursed her lips and shook his head. "You never forget anything."

Travis shrugged. It wasn't that odd, considering his reaction to meeting Jaron.

He stood and walked to the back door, pulling on his boots. "I'll go get them."

"Who did you hire for me?" Beverly asked.

"I didn't hire him. Just told him to call you." Travis had his hand on the doorknob. "You know Gloria McAllister's son."

"Gloria talks about Jaron all the time."

"Yeah. Turns out he wasn't missing at all. He's back in town and needs a job." Travis wanted to ask his mother to hire Jaron so he'd get to see him every day but maybe that wasn't a good idea since he didn't have a fucking clue what he should do about his attraction.

Everything about Jaron called to some protective instinct Travis wasn't aware he even had until meeting him. He couldn't help but want to wrap his arms around Jaron and never let go, shield him from the world. Maybe that was what had him all twisted up in knots. Lord knew he'd never felt like that about anyone else in the whole of his life. He was too self-absorbed in high school to pay attention to someone like Jaron.

He had just turned the doorknob when Elmer, one of his farm hands, crossed the backyard. "It's Maggie. She looks like she's having contractions."

Travis was out of the door in a second, with Greg right behind him.

"She's early." Greg's presence beside him calmed Travis some. The kid remembered everything he ever read and had a love for animals. He read everything he could on horses because he thought it was a fun topic, which made him almost as good as having a veterinarian there.

"Yeah." Everything left his mind except Maggie.

Chapter Eight

♥

Jaron's hands shook when he stepped into the backyard, cell phone in hand.

Bobby giggled from inside the kitchen, where he helped Gloria make dinner.

Jaron used the word *helped* loosely. Didn't matter how it tasted. Jaron would eat it with a smile on his face because Bobby didn't need him in the room while he *helped* and that was progress.

Whatever lasting trauma Bobby had from witnessing Tracy's death, they would both get help after they settled into their new life. He would take small steps until then. Bobby not needing Jaron in the room was a giant leap. Or it felt like one from where Jaron stood without Bobby hugging his leg with his thumb in his mouth. Maybe his little boy wouldn't suffer long term. Maybe they'd both be okay.

If Bobby could leap toward the positive, then Jaron would lose the nerves and call Beverly Heath for that job Travis mentioned.

He dialed her number, having memorized it earlier. It rang twice before someone answered. "Hello." The woman sounded as if she had hit and passed middle age a few years ago.

"Hi. I'm Jaron McAllister. Travis told me to call you about a house-cleaning position."

"Yes, dear. I'm looking for someone to clean, of course, but also can you cook?"

"I was a short order cook for my last job. I'm not a chef or anything, though."

Beverly chuckled. "No creativity required, young man. Just a sandwich and maybe breakfast on occasion."

"That I can do." He smiled and sighed, losing some of the tension in his body before he even knew he had any.

"Are you able to come by tomorrow? 8 o'clock in the morning, perhaps?"

Up until that moment, Jaron hadn't thought about finding a sitter for Bobby. He'd have to think of something when and if Beverly hired him. Since tomorrow was Saturday, his mom could probably sit with Bobby. If Bobby would stay. Being able to leave the room and putting miles between them seemed like a stretch. Should he push it?

"Hmm. Yeah, I can come by at that time."

"All right, dear. I'll see you tomorrow morning."

They hung up after that. Jaron stuffed the phone into his jeans pocket and turned to enter the house.

His mom and Bobby were at the counter, mixing something in a bowl. Bobby stood on a kitchen chair. She'd never smiled as much when he was younger as she did with Bobby. Or maybe he just didn't remember. He remembered her working all the time and not much else. That smile was a good change.

He tugged on his mom's shirt, getting her attention. "Can you..." He pointed to Bobby. "Tomorrow. Interview with Beverly Heath."

Mom waved him away. "Of course. But will he stay with me?"

Jaron made a face and shrugged. He moved to Bobby's other side and peered into the bowl. "What are you making?"

Instead of answering, Bobby looked to Gloria for guidance. She answered for him. "Mashed potatoes for shepherds pie."

"Well, that sounds very yummy."

"Grandma says I can help her all the time."

Jaron smiled. "You're a big helper."

"I know. I told her."

"Tried to sell yourself, did ya."

Mom chuckled and ruffled Bobby's hair. "You did a fine job."

Jaron took a deep breath, gearing himself up for the next conversation. "You know that man we met at the grocery store?"

Bobby nodded.

"Well, I have to go to his house tomorrow morning."

Bobby shrugged. "How come?"

"His family might give me a job. I have to go talk to them about that."

Bobby drew his eyebrows together, and he stopped stirring. He turned to Jaron. "I can't come?"

Oh God, there it was, and Jaron had no idea how to approach the situation. He did the only thing he knew wouldn't be a mistake. "Not this time, snuggle bear."

"Does Grandma have to go too?"

Hm. "No."

His mom smiled at Bobby. "How about we let your dad have his boring talks, and we go to the zoo?"

Bobby's eyes lit up, and he nodded. "We can see penguins?"

"I'm not sure if the zoo has penguins, but if they do, then we can watch them for as long as you want."

Jaron reached over to get her attention. "Thanks, Mom."

She nodded. "Bev's a good friend of mine."

That hadn't been the case when Jaron left. "I didn't know that."

"Willis dying did a number on that family. I had something in common with Bev." She gave him an accusing look and Jaron knew she meant when he'd left.

Instead of engaging in an argument in front of Bobby, Jaron decided to take the high road. "Glad you were able to make a connection."

"Yes well, I'm telling you because she'll bring up your disappearance."

Disappearance?

From her point of view, he had disappeared. As a parent, he completely understood that. "Did you ever try to look for me?"

Mom nodded. "I talked to Brian, and I went to the police. He wouldn't do anything because you were technically an adult and left on your own."

"I took the bus to Bellcroft at first. Stayed about a year. Just long enough to figure out the place wasn't for me. Got a job at a restaurant working in the kitchen while I was there. When I put my two-week notice in, I explained to the restaurant owner why I was leaving. It just so happened that he knew Connie, who owned a diner in Palina. He put in a good word for me, and I moved there. I met Tracy. She was pregnant with this guy at the time." Jaron smiled and ruffled Bobby's hair. "Tracy and I needed each other, I think. We became a family. Then she died, and here I am."

"What did you need from her that you didn't get here?" Mom bit out the question as if it held all kinds of accusations.

Jaron had to push down the anger, which took a moment longer than his mom liked if the look on her face was any indication. "I think she knew she wouldn't be a good parent and she needed me to step up. For me, she mostly gave me acceptance. She loved me unconditionally." Jaron smiled and fought to hold back tears. "She loved everyone like that. Judged no one. She was a free-spirit."

Mom didn't speak, but held his gaze, for so long Jaron grew un-comfortable. "You felt judged and unloved here?"

"Yes. Very much so."

Mom turned away, looking at the half-mashed potatoes in the bowl. Her face turned red right before she started crying.

Chapter Nine

C hapter Nine

The Heath farm lay about ten minutes away on the east side of Pickleville. His mom let Jaron borrow the car. He hadn't driven in years, having driven Andrew home from the bar when he'd gotten too drunk to drive himself once, but that had been years ago. Cars were needed around Pickleville as public transportation wasn't a thing. Not like in the city where no one needed to drive because things were either close enough to walk to or close to the trains and buses.

Jaron drove with the windows rolled down, taking in the fresh air, passing unharvested fields, orchards, and forests in equal measure. The air was ripe with peaches and still-green apples, along with decaying leaves leftover from last fall. Nature at its finest, something the city didn't have much of, and Jaron only realized how much he'd missed that one thing. Jaron had forgotten about Pickleville's wide-open spaces and acres of forest. Or maybe he'd never really seen the spaces, between his rebellious immaturity and the lack of acceptance.

The pavement gave way to dirt, and the forest turned into a swampy marsh. Gravel crunched under tires, and he slowed down, not wanting to slide around. One pebble wasn't a problem, but a bunch together made the gravel road slicker than pavement. The air smelled slightly of fish, and frogs chirped out their protest at the intrusion.

The green of summer hadn't given over to fall's colors, and with the warm air, Jaron had the illusion summer would never end.

When did the tall buildings and all those people in the big city begin to make him feel closed up? Not closed *in*. Not claustrophobic. But closed *up* like a locked closet. When he'd first moved, he felt as if his whole life waited there amongst the steel and concrete, ready to begin something extraordinary, make connections with people.

Tracy had been bigger than life and so extroverted she'd taken the meaning of that word to the next level. The only thing he and Andrew had had in common was the fact that they were gay. They were different in every other way. Jaron loved that Andrew mixed up his English and Spanish a lot, and that he had the tough, observant cop thing down so thoroughly that it was instinct.

It took him less time to realize that no one would hand him whatever he needed to make his life easier the way his mother had, not even Tracy and Andrew. He had thought he'd get off the bus and everyone would stand at the city gates with smiles and open arms, taking him into the fold. Instead, everyone moved around him as if he were a ghost.

Pickleville's small, gossipy atmosphere held problems of its own—nothing like the city. Could he live with the problems in Pickleville? The bigger question was how the problems in Pickleville would affect Bobby. He wanted Bobby to have the best life possible but wasn't sure if he'd made the right decision moving or not. He had a feeling he'd find out sooner rather than later.

Travis Heath hadn't exactly been his friend in high school, so he hadn't ever been to the farm before. Everything he knew about it, he'd learned through gossip in the high school hallways. He'd heard bits and pieces of factual information in amongst everything else, but he managed to get enough of the puzzle to know the Heaths owned most of the land in Pickleville, making them the biggest farmers around. He knew they raised cattle and horses. Since he passed enough of the Heath's fields on the way there, he also knew they grew some fruits and vegetables as well.

The driveway curved around a house so big, Jaron understood why Beverly needed someone to clean. No way could one person take care of something so big, and Beverly was as old as Gloria, which didn't make her ancient, but she was probably slowing down a bit. The white house had two stories and an extra wing on each side, making it look like a giant *u*.

He wondered if Travis still lived at home. The house was so big, he'd never see Beverly if he didn't want to. Still, everyone their age wanted out from under their parents' roof and rules, not that Travis had a whole lot of those in his life, if the rumors meant anything.

Several outbuildings were scattered around the property, all painted red with white trim. A circular corral sat in front of a barn on the right. There was a horse inside, standing near the fence with its eyes half-closed.

He parked the car next to a gray truck, rolling up the window before shutting off the engine. Opening and closing the car door didn't seem to faze the sleeping horse even a little bit. He pocketed his keys as he walked to the front door of the house. He ran his hands down his jean-covered thighs and took a deep breath before he knocked.

Beverly opened the door with a smile. He had seen her around town a few times before he'd moved, so he had an image in his mind. Despite a different hairstyle, how he remembered her wasn't very far off the mark.

He held out his hand and introduced himself. "Hello, I'm Jaron McAllister."

"I know, dear." Beverly took his hand between both of hers, patting him. Her hands were soft as if she just moisturized them with some expensive lotion. Travis had the same colored eyes, except his held mischief, where hers didn't. "Come in. And we'll get you started."

She walked him through the downstairs, explaining what she needed. The antiques scattered around, coupled with his clumsiness, scared him more than he would ever admit. She told him about how long he should expect to take in each room once he found his momentum. "The upstairs is where I would like you to start first. That's probably the worst of the mess."

He expected an interview with lots of questions, but he found himself dusting the last room on the hallway's left side.

He stood outside a closed door, knocking to make sure no one occupied the room. He knocked on every room that had a closed door. "Hello. Housekeeper coming in. Brace yourself."

All the rooms in the east wing had been empty so far. He didn't expect anything different from that one, which was why he didn't wait for anyone to answer but went right in, humming a song he had heard on a commercial last night. Damn thing had gotten stuck in his head to the point he didn't know how to get rid of it.

The song evaporated like smoke when he saw a naked ass. He sucked in a breath right before he yelled, "Oh my God." His voice sounded loud even to his own ears, especially in the dark room where someone had pulled the thick curtains closed to shut out the light.

Travis lay on his stomach sprawled across the bed, which sat in the middle of the room against the far wall. He looked like a framed photo, all perfect and peaceful. Pornographic in the most artistic way possible.

Jaron adjusted the hard-on in his pants and took a deep breath before his brain started functioning again.

So should he leave or continue cleaning?

Jaron decided he probably should leave.

He walked backward to get as long a look as possible at that perfect body. And promptly tripped over a pile of clothing he didn't remember stepping around to get inside the room. The horse in the round fence thingy probably heard the *crunch* his plastic cleaning caddy made and the *boom* of him falling backward on his ass. His cleaning supplies went everywhere, bottles lay beside him instead of underneath as the caddy went sideways right before he landed. How the caddy ended up underneath him, he didn't know, but a sharp piece of plastic stuck into his ass.

Travis came off the bed with a jolt and a curse. "What the fuck?"

He looked around the room, trying to find the answer to the crudely worded question. When his gaze landed on Jaron, he found it. He ran a hand down his face. "Shit, you scared me."

"Sorry."

Travis smiled and rose from the bed in all his naked glory, squatting down beside him. He took a cleaning bottle from Jaron's hand. Jaron hadn't even known he'd held it. "Are you okay?"

Heat crept into his cheeks, but he smiled, trying to brush off the embarrassment. "My pride is bruised but other than that I'm fine."

Travis chuckled. "Mom gave you the job already, I see."

"Can we have this conversation when you're clothed, please?" Jaron looked directly at the man's gorgeous cock when he said it. The thing held Jaron's attention for sure and would hold it until Travis got dressed. Since he didn't feel like getting his ass kicked for taking a peek, Travis should cover himself, even though, doing so was a shame.

Travis' eyes sparkled with mischief. "What would be the fun in that?"

Jaron's eyes widened. Was that flirting?

Travis pulled him to his feet and stepped away.

He stood there, watching as Travis rummaged around in his dresser, searching for clothing. At least Jaron hoped he intended to cover himself. Okay, Jaron rode the fence on whether or not he wanted Travis to get dressed because who wouldn't want to see that for the rest of the day. Or longer. Whatever.

"Shit."

"What?"

"No clean underwear."

Jaron groaned, closing his eyes so he could get his dick to calm the fuck down. That was not an invitation.

"I can start some laundry for you. It will take a while, though."

"You don't have to do that. You are not my servant or anything."

Can't I be, please? Oh please. "It's okay. I don't mind."

He picked up his cleaning supplies and stacked them against the wall, so they were out of his way before leaving the room to get a trash can to toss out the broken caddy. By the time he came back, Travis wasn't anywhere in sight.

He wasn't sure if he should've been sad about that or not.

Jaron had started on lunch when Beverly came into the kitchen. "Jaron, can I talk to you, please?"

"Sure." He washed his hands and followed her to the library. Or he guessed that's what they called it on account of all the books in the room.

"Travis told me you went into his room earlier." She sat down on a plush chair and indicated Jaron should sit as well.

Jaron chose the couch. "I'm sorry, ma'am. I didn't know whether to go in or not. I knocked, I swear."

"Oh, it's me that wants to apologize. I completely forgot that Travis slept here. He got in very late last night."

Jaron just bet he did. "It's okay. I promise to knock louder next time."

Beverly laughed. "I'm sure you got an eyeful."

Oh God, how embarrassing. He looked down, enthralled with the neat little swirls in the carpet. "I broke your cleaning thing when I fell."

"That's fine, dear. As long as you're okay." When he met her gaze again, she smiled.

Jaron nodded and then wrung his hands when she studied him, not speaking for the longest time. He didn't know whether to get up and continue lunch preparations or sit there until she excused him. Sitting there regressed him to his childhood days, making him feel as if he were under scrutiny.

He cleared his throat, and that seemed to do the trick as she spoke again. "You've done a great job so far. How do you feel about a permanent position?"

Jaron smiled. "I'll take it, ma'am." His smile fell, and he thought of his transportation issues. "I have transportation issues at the moment, though."

"You can either move in here. We have plenty of room, and my last housekeeper lived here. Or I can send a farmhand to pick you up."

"I don't know if I feel comfortable moving my son again so soon."

"Gloria told me about Bobby. He could ride the bus here from school instead of at Gloria's house if you'd like. I'm sure he'd like learning to ride horses and exploring the farm. We have plenty of people around to keep an eye on him."

"Bobby's not in school yet."

Beverly drew her eyebrows together. "I believe the school year has already started. You should enroll him very soon."

Jaron sighed. His shoulders slumped. "I know." Whatever nervousness he'd felt around her disappeared, and he found himself unloading on her a bit. "I do know, I swear. But the kids in this town weren't very nice to me while I was growing up and I don't know if that's changed. It scares me to put my son in a similar situation."

"Travis wasn't cruel to you? His father would have had a fit if he knew he picked on someone for being gay. For any reason for that matter."

"No. Travis wasn't. His friends, Jackson and Brad were the worst. The other kids just shunned me and gossiped."

"I don't know how things are anymore, but I do know there are some in town who are gay. My friend, Karen and her wife. They haven't had any trouble at all."

Jaron sighed with relief. "That's great."

She smiled. "So what else is bothering you about your son and starting school?"

"Bobby will throw a fit the second he sees the classroom and...I'm a coward."

Beverly chuckled. "And maybe you're a father who doesn't want to let go of his baby just yet."

Jaron smiled. "And that, yeah."

Jaron felt a million pounds lighter after talking to Beverly. A lot of it had to do with him having a steady flow of income. He might live with his mother, but he didn't mooch off her. He had given her money every week he'd been there since moving in, and he intended to keep doing that until he moved out, not that he had a plan to do that anytime soon, despite Beverly's offer.

A little part of his relief had been talking to Beverly about Bobby. However brief the conversation, he'd needed to get his worries off his chest.

He piled two ham and cheese sandwiches with vegetables and added a side plate of fruit to each one, setting them on the kitchen table.

Travis came through the kitchen door just as Jaron set a glass of lemonade beside each serving.

"Wash up. Eat." The comment came out sharp and biting, and even he didn't know why.

"Yes, sir." Travis smiled before disappearing. He wasn't gone but a couple of minutes. He nodded to one of the place settings. "One of those for me?"

"Of course." The question seemed odd, but Jaron didn't want to start a conversation with Travis. He'd rather let him eat and do something else in another part of the house.

Travis sat down. "This looks good. Thank you." Jaron didn't reply, not even to be polite. Instead, he headed to the door that led into the hallway. "Aren't you eating?"

"No."

Beverly chose that moment to come into the room but from the opposite door. Travis took advantage of that and told on him. "Mom, Jaron isn't eating." Jaron stopped with his hand on the door and glared at Travis, who had a smug expression. The bastard.

Beverly gave him the mom stare. "Why not?"

"Just not hungry, Ma'am."

"Oh now, sit down and eat. You worked hard all morning."

Jaron sighed and went over to the kitchen island again, making himself a sandwich.

"How are Maggie and the baby, dear?" Beverly asked Travis. The whole time Travis watched Jaron.

"Doing good this morning, Mom." Travis took another bite of his sandwich and winked at Jaron when he caught him looking.

Jaron blushed.

"It's a good thing Elmer was in the barn when she started having trouble."

Travis nodded his head. "Greg's the one that saved the colt's life. The kid is smart, Mom. We should help him pay for college if he wants to go."

Beverly nodded. "Of course. Greg is family now, after all."

Jaron didn't know who they spoke of, but he thought it was super-generous that they would pay for someone's college tuition. Jaron finished making a sandwich and carried it to the table before going back for a glass of lemonade.

"Can I ask a question?" Jaron sat down and took a bite of his sandwich.

"Shoot." Travis watched him.

"Maggie and the baby?" Their conversation made them sound nonhuman. Knowing the kinds of animals on the farm, Jaron would guess a cow or horse. Bobby would love seeing a baby animal, regardless of what kind.

"Horses." Travis smiled.

"Mind if I bring Bobby by to see them sometime?"

"Anytime." Travis' expression softened.

No way was Travis looking at Jaron's mouth as if he wanted to see his lips wrapped around something other than a sandwich.

"What?" Jaron wasn't interpreting that look correctly. Was he?

"What?"

"Knock it off."

"What am I doing?" Travis' eyes sparkled with mischief.

"You're watching me eat. It's creepy. So quit."

As they bantered back and forth, Beverly looked as if she were watching tennis.

"I can't."

"Yes, you can. I have faith in your ability to be noncreepy."

"Non-creepy? Is that even a word?"

"It is now."

"You are something else. You know that? You like making friends. I can tell. For some reason, you don't want to with me. Why is that?"

Shit. He hadn't realized he'd been that transparent. "Are you trying to make me angry?"

"Yes, I'm trying to make you angry." Travis outright chuckled.

"Why?"

"Because you are so damn cute right now."

Jaron's head snapped back. If Travis had slapped him, it would have had less of an impact. He stood, excusing himself as he practically ran out of the room. He headed down the hall that led to the stairs and to the laundry room. He pulled clothes out of the dryer and set them on the folding table.

Travis was a walking, talking heartbreak and a temptation Jaron couldn't afford.

He told himself to breathe and forget about Travis. The only problem was, Jaron held the man's underwear in his hands.

Chapter Ten

♥

M aybe Jaron read more into what Travis had said at lunch than was there. He lay in bed staring up at the ceiling, going over the entire conversation in his mind, only he thought about the thousands of things he should have said instead of running away.

Maybe Travis hadn't meant anything by it other than making fun of Jaron, just like in high school. Although Travis had never, most of his friends had. Maybe nothing had changed in the town but him. And he *had* changed. He'd grown up enough not to stand by and take the crap others spewed his way. He understood that what other people thought of him wasn't any of his business, and he liked it that way. But even if Travis was making fun of him and the flirting was all one big prank, Jaron was still attracted to Travis. He felt helpless in the face of that and didn't know how to protect himself.

Jaron's phone chirped, indicating he had a text. The light on the phone came on, illuminating the dark room. Jaron looked down at Bobby's sleeping body. He put the phone on vibrate before checking the small screen.

Can't sleep. Wondering if u r up 2. Travis.

Yep. God, Jaron was hopeless. Why did he text back?

Can I come over? What was the man's motivation? Knowing that would solve a lot of Jaron's problems.

2 am and you'll wake Bobby.

I'll b quiet.

What do u want?

Can we have this conversation face to face?

Guess so.

Will u come outside?

Well, shit. *Ur outside my door aren't u?*

Lol. Yeah.

Jaron told himself a thousand reasons why going outside to meet up with Travis was a bad idea. Travis would break his heart before the end. One way or another, that was inevitable. Jaron knew it, and probably Travis knew it too. So why, oh why was he going outside in the dark with bugs that wanted to suck his blood and a man who may or may not want to suck something else? Why?

Jaron got out of bed and grabbed a pair of pajama pants that had purple and green plaid stripes on them. He tiptoed through the house as if he was a teenager. Okay, well, he was sneaking out. But he was an adult, damn it. He could leave if he wanted. Even if he did live with his mother and she would flip the fuck out if she knew he'd met a guy out on the street.

He slipped out of the back door and made his way to the front of the house. Searching around in the dark, he discovered Travis' truck across the street.

The pavement felt cool beneath his bare feet as he closed the distance between them. The air was just cold enough to raise goose bumps on his naked chest.

Crickets and frogs fought in the dark to see who could make the best night sounds.

Travis sat in his truck with the driver's side window rolled down and his arm resting on the window's edge. He had on the same clothes as he'd had on at lunch.

Jaron folded his arms over his chest. "Creepy much. What if I hadn't been awake?"

"Wouldn't have mattered. I haven't been able to think about anything or anyone else since I met you. Well, re-met you." Jaron hadn't seen such a serious side to Travis. Not that he knew much about him but gone was the mischievous playboy with the killer smile. In his place was a man who looked as if he had something important on his mind.

Jaron didn't know what to say. He watched the streetlights reflect off the shiny black surface of the truck, making pictures in the shine.

"Why does that scare you?" Travis watched Jaron. Jaron could feel his gaze burn into him.

"I could ask you the same thing." Jaron knew what scared him about Travis' flirtatious advances.

"I'm not out, Jaron. Hell, before you came into town, I had no intention of coming out."

An uncomfortable silence fell between them. For Jaron, being gay was something that came along at birth. Like having brown hair. Just another part of him. Jaron had always known who he was and what that meant for him. Finding men attractive was a small part of the bigger whole. "Are you looking for advice here? Because I don't have any other than to say, life is better when you live it authentically."

Travis smiled for the first time since they'd started their nighttime chat. "Is that why you came out in high school?"

"It was middle school actually and no. Brad Flynn outed me when he caught me looking at his dick." Jaron rolled his eyes. He had thought everyone knew that story. "No one should be forced out the way I was, which is why I'll just say we can pretend this conversation never happened and go our separate ways."

"No. I don't want that."

"Well, what then, Travis?" Jaron looked up at Travis, at the intensity in his eyes, and decided to lay it on the line. "I can't do casual. I have a kid that doesn't need that kind of inconsistency from me. He got enough of that from his mother." Jaron dragged his hands through his hair and laughed sardonically. "Do you even know why I moved back here?"

"No."

"Bobby's mother and her biker boyfriend killed each other. Bobby was in the room when it happened. I found them in my living room, and Bobby under the blankets on my bed."

Travis opened the door to his truck. Jaron moved out of the way. The minute Travis was clear of the door he pulled Jaron into his arms, hugging him.

"God, baby, I am so sorry."

"Tracy was a crappy mom, but she loved Bobby." Jaron hugged him back for a minute, just enjoying the heat the other man gave off. Jaron stuck his face in Travis shirt-covered chest. He smelled good, like soap and something distinctly Travis that Jaron couldn't name. Jaron sighed and let him go.

Travis took a step toward his truck. "I've never dated anyone seriously before. Don't know if I want to."

Travis' honesty shouldn't have caused an ache in his chest, but it did. He folded his arms around his middle and took a step back. "I understand."

"I didn't say that to hurt your feelings."

Jaron's gaze snapped to his, and his eyes narrowed. "You didn't."

Travis gave him a disbelieving look, but he didn't continue down the path that would start an argument. "I'm just saying I need time to consider things."

Jaron rolled his eyes. "I'm not one of the girls in this town who throws themselves at you just because you're handsome and charming. I'm not waiting in a tower for you to make up your mind whether or not you want to save me. I can and have saved myself."

Travis raised his eyebrows, and a slight smile turned up the corners of his mouth.

He didn't say anything, but Jaron knew the thoughts in his head as they'd had that same conversation once before. Travis might think him cute when angry, but he didn't feel cute. "Shut up."

"Okay." Travis' smile broadened.

Jaron sighed and turned to go back into the house. "Go home, Travis. Find some girl to fuck and forget we ever had this conversation."

"I never said I wouldn't date you."

Jaron shook his head and waved a hand. "And I never said I *would* date *you*, so don't think you have me on a string."

"Are you saying you don't want to date?"

Jaron made it to the middle of his yard before he stopped and turned. "I'm saying you're right. You have a lot to think about, and none of that has anything to do with me."

That must have been what Travis needed to hear because he nodded and got in his truck. He gave Jaron one last look before he drove off.

Chapter Eleven

♥

Bobby clung to Jaron as they sat in the elementary school's office and Jaron felt like doing the same. School held a level of panic he didn't expect to feel, and he wasn't even the one going. Because it was his kid, made it even worse, though. His chest tightened and he tried not to picture Bobby getting bullied. It didn't matter the reason for the bullying. Jaron's mind still conjured up the images.

"How do you handle bullying?" Jaron gave the principal a pointed look.

"We have a zero tolerance for it district wide. I can't say in never happens but when it does, an adult mediates a verbal exchange between all the children involved. Our goal is to empower the student to stick up for himself."

Jaron narrowed his eyes. He wasn't about to believe that right away. She had a lot to prove. The entire Pickleville school district did. "When I went here, teachers didn't do anything about it."

She nodded and smiled. "I taught kindergarten at that time, so I wasn't sure what went on at the high school. But I'm aware of your situation Mr. McAllister. Since you've graduated, we've added a zero-tolerance policy and I know there is a gay-straight alliance at the high school. My son is a part of it. I can reassure you, bullying for any reason isn't something we take lightly. Not anymore."

Jaron nodded. He'd never expected that. "Who started the alliance?"

"Miss Larson. And I personally am grateful she did."

Jaron smiled for the first time since walking in. Some of the tension went out of his shoulders and the panic eased.

And then Bobby scooted closer to him.

Jaron might as well have found a pirate ship and made Bobby walk the plank with sharks swimming at the bottom, anticipating the tenderness of such young lunch. Bobby would find that a better experience than starting school.

Jaron looked down at those blue eyes. They pleaded with him to not make him do the dreaded thing.

Don't cave. "You'll make so many friends and have fun. You'll see."

"Okay, Mr. McAllister. We need you to fill out these papers. If you'd like, I can take Bobby to his class."

"No Papa." Bobby's grip on his leg tightened.

Bobby's lip quivered and his eyes filled with tears. Then Jaron met the school principal's gaze and shook his head. "He won't go with you. I'll take him and then come back to finish these."

Her smile suggested she'd had experience with clingy children and emotional parents before. "It's Ms. Larson's class. Two doors down on the right."

"Ms. Larson is Bobby's teacher?" Lucky break.

The principal smiled. "That's right. When she got her certification in elementary education, the school district moved her over to a kindergarten classroom. At her request."

Jaron didn't know or care what kind of hoops Ms. Larson had to jump through to teach younger children. He was just glad she did. "She was my favorite teacher."

"I'm sure she'd like to hear that."

"I'll let her know then. Thanks." He pried Bobby's hand off his leg and held it as they walked out of the office.

"Do I have to go in there?"

Jaron fought the urge to chuckle. "Yes, you have to go in there. There are other kids in there to play with."

"So."

"So, the teacher is nice too. She taught me when I was in school, and now I know all kinds of stuff."

"I don't care."

"Yeah, I get that. But I do care. I want you to learn and get smart, so someday you can take care of me. I want a yellow mansion and a blue sports car and a green dog that I'm going to call Booger."

Bobby laughed. "How am I gonna get that?"

"You learn how to read and write and add numbers."

"Then what?"

"Let's start with those three things, okay. One step at a time."

"That's what I'm gonna learn in there?" Bobby pointed to the door, looking at it as if it was a big disgusting pile of dog crap.

"Yep. It'll be fun."

"I don't think so."

"Just try it."

"Why can't you teach me?"

"Bobby," Jaron sighed in exasperation. He met Bobby's gaze. "So here's what's gonna happen. I'm gonna knock on the door, and we'll both go in together."

"I have to?"

"Yes."

Bobby took a deep breath, shoring up his courage and nodded. "Okay."

Thank God. A small step but still in the right direction.

Jaron knocked, avoiding the colorful poster taped to the door that read *Ms. Larson's class is cool*.

Ms. Larson stood there, smiling at them. Seven years hadn't aged her much, but then she wasn't that much older than Jaron if how she appeared was any indication. "You must be Robert."

Bobby clung to Jaron's leg again and turned his head in the opposite direction. "That's not my name."

"We call him Bobby."

"Why don't you both come in? For the first few minutes of the day, we have free time, which means you can play wherever you'd like." She met Jaron's gaze. "You're welcome to stay for the day if you'd like."

Jaron had to practically pry Bobby off his leg to enter the classroom. Once they got inside, he clung again, but hearing the other kids playing around the room piqued his interest. His body slowly relaxed until he merely leaned against Jaron with his thumb in his mouth.

Jaron decided to let Bobby settle in on his own. Not focusing on Bobby's negative reaction wouldn't highlight it and bring it back to the surface again. Instead, he met Ms. Larson's gaze. "I don't know if you remember me."

She nodded. "Jaron McAllister. I remember."

"Lucky break for Bobby that you're his teacher."

Ms. Larson chuckled. "I'm glad you think so. And I'm glad you're back in town."

"Thanks. Being back has been...surprisingly great."

"I bet, since you received the brunt end of the bullying in high school."

"That I did, Ms. Larson."

"You can call me Beth." Beth's gaze traveled the room in watchful circles over and over again, making sure the kids played safely. "Excuse me a minute. Don't go anywhere." She walked over to a little boy who held a big, waffle type block over his head. She knelt, getting on the kid's level before she spoke to him. She kept their conversation private, but whatever she said made the boy set the block down on the carpet and move to another area of the classroom. Beth came back. "Are you planning on stay in town for good?"

Bobby eased away from him, playing with small blocks on the floor with a dark-haired boy. The other kid handed a red block to Bobby, and that seemed to start their friendship. "I'm making a horse 'cuz my Daddy just got a new horse for us to ride."

Bobby didn't say anything back, but he gave the other boy his full attention.

"I think so. I haven't decided yet. I suppose it depends on how homophobic the town still is. I don't want Bobby raised around people like that."

"I don't know if you're aware, but I gave Jackson and Brad detention as much as I possibly could."

Jaron cleared his throat as he let that information sink into his soul. The implications of that one thing coupled with experiences with Beverly being so kind changed Jaron's perspective. He also couldn't deny Travis' kindness. "No, I-I didn't know that."

Jaron had seen Pickleville as a dark pit during most of his high school years. He'd had the whole no-one-understands-me thing down to a science. That had blackened his perspective until he'd painted everyone with the same brush.

"Most people around here are decent. And our LGBT community is growing slowly every year. The town is better than before."

"I think I'm starting to see that."

She smiled. "I'm glad to hear it. If you have time some weekend, we could catch up sometime."

Jaron smiled a real, genuine smile for the first time in a long while. He'd almost forgotten how. "I would like that."

"Let me get your number, and I'll call you." She walked over to a short, round table that sat in one corner of the room and grabbed a pad of paper and a pencil. She closed the distance between them again. "I have to get the class started, or I'd stand here talking all day."

Jaron took the paper and pencil from her and wrote his number down before giving them back to her.

"And I have to sneak out of here to go to work." Jaron turned his gaze to Bobby. He had several blocks stacked on top of each other until a colorful wall formed.

Jaron bit his lip and met Beth's gaze again. "Sneaking out is the right approach, right? Or will I create even more abandonment issues." Shit. He didn't know what to do.

"You know your son better than anyone, so you do what you think is best."

While that was a very good answer, it didn't help him at all.

The short, squatty bookcase stood between him and Bobby. He purposefully kept it between them as he spoke. "Papa's leaving. Grandma's going to get off work early and pick you up." As much as Jaron wanted Bobby to ride the bus to the Heath farm, he thought letting Bobby settle into the routine of school for a week or two would prove less stressful for them both. Thank God for his mom. If it weren't for her, Jaron and Bobby would have had a much harder time.

Bobby didn't pay any attention to him. His sole focus was on the wall made out of blocks. He nodded, though, so Jaron knew Bobby had heard him. Jaron turned to Beth. "My mom's coming to pick him up." She already knew that because he had just said it, but his stomach ached at the thought of leaving Bobby.

Beth gave him a knowing smiled. "Bobby will be just fine."

"Yeah. Okay." But what if Bobby started crying and Jaron wasn't there to help him through? "I know."

Jaron waved as he walked out of the classroom, letting Beth get her class started. He sat in the office filling out the rest of the forms, which took a whole ten minutes and handed them to the secretary right before he left the school.

Jaron felt the need to cry down to the bottom of his stomach during the walk back to his mom's house. He waited until after he called Beverly. He had a good ten minutes before his ride showed up. He hoped it was enough time to get it all out of his system.

He grabbed a few tissues from the box in the bathroom before heading out of the door, waiting in his driveway so whoever picked him up didn't have to bother shutting off the truck. They probably had as much work on the farm as Jaron did in the house. He was eager to get started.

He wiped his eyes and blew his nose when a gray truck pulled into the driveway. He didn't know the older man behind the wheel but his status as a farmhand came through in the way he dressed. He had a long-sleeved shirt, and a dirty cap advertising a truck manufacturer.

Jaron smiled at the man as he got in the truck. "Thanks for picking me up." Jaron needed a car in a bad way. Or he needed to take Beverly up on her offer to live there on the farm. Because asking the farmhands to pick him up every day seemed a bit much.

"Don't think I'm gonna be doin' this again. I don't like faggots in my truck."

Jaron tensed, not seeing that coming from someone who worked for Beverly, who was such a kind lady.

The good experience at the school and the way he was into his own emotions was enough not to notice the sneer on the guy's face. If he had, he wouldn't have accepted a ride from him.

He moved as close to the door as possible and looked out of the window, hoping the guy wouldn't speak to him again or do anything violent.

Jaron thought about getting out of the truck, but the guy put it in reverse before he could make up his mind.

The ride remained silent except for the country music coming from the radio.

Jaron couldn't help but wonder how many other people on Travis' farm shared the same attitude.

Between reconnecting with Beth and getting called a filthy name, his day just balanced itself out. All of that paled in comparison to the emotional crisis that was his baby starting school for the first time.

Chapter Twelve

C **hapter Twelve**

Travis came out of the barn and saw Jaron come around the corner of the house with a rug in one hand and a broom in the other. He headed for the clothesline in the side yard. He hadn't seen anyone use it in so long he barely remembered it was there.

Travis leaned against the barn and watched as Jaron threw the rug over the line until it folded in half. Once he was satisfied it would stay on, he beat the shit out of it with the broom.

It wasn't until Jaron turned his head, putting his whole body into the whack that he saw the red around Jaron's eyes and the blotchy patches on his cheeks.

Travis stiffened as he stood from his leaning position. It had been a long time since he'd lost his temper. Not since his father had died and he'd needed somewhere to put the grief, so he'd started a fist fight with Brad that had ended with both of them bloody and bruised but still friends.

Greg came out of the cow barn, took one look at Travis, and did a one-eighty turn, going back the way he came. Smart kid. Smarter than most.

Travis closed the distance between himself and Jaron, grabbing his arm once he got close enough. Jaron turned, raising the broom like a weapon before he lowered it again. "What?"

Travis knew enough about Jaron to know he wasn't a fighter. He wasn't the type to look over his shoulder at every turn, despite the bullying he'd endured in high school. He wouldn't have weaponized the broom unless something had happened.

"Who made you cry?"

"Bobby started school for the first time today. I'm being weird about it, is all."

Travis let go of his arm. If he held on any longer, he'd pull him into a hug. As much as he wanted that, he needed to remember their conversation from Saturday night. Jaron all but told him to get his shit together before making any romantic gestures toward him. A hug was as platonic as it came with anyone else. Not Jaron.

"Did anyone try to hurt you?"

Jaron averted his gaze to the ground before he turned back to the rug. "No."

Travis clenched his jaw to keep from snapping at Jaron. Something had already happened and Travis losing his shit all over the poor guy wouldn't help the situation. "Just tell me what happened."

Jaron's shoulders came up to his ears. "It's not a big deal. Just got called a name. Nothing I haven't been through before."

"Who was it?"

"The guy who picked me up today."

Jesus, getting answers was like pulling teeth. "What do you mean? Who picked you up?"

Jaron shrugged. "I didn't take the time to get to know the guy, and I'll steer clear while I'm here. It's not a big deal."

Travis stiffened. "Mom had one of my hands pick you up?"

"Yeah, but I'll figure something else out from now on. Not fair to take them away from their work even long enough to give me a ride."

Travis turned toward the house. "I don't give a fuck about interrupting their day, Jaron."

He didn't wait for Jaron to respond. He'd learned enough to know Jaron didn't mind arguing. They'd both stand there pushing each other's buttons until they grew old if he didn't walk away sooner rather than later. He had a situation to correct anyway.

Travis found his mother behind the desk in the library. He knocked on the side of the open door to get her attention. She looked up from her computer and met his eyes. "What happened?" His mother did know him best, after all. His expression must have been harsh.

"Who did you send to get Jaron?"

"Elmer. Why?"

"Called Jaron a name. I'll take care of it." Travis turned from the room. The urgency to get Elmer off his property and away from Jaron sent adrenaline through his system. His heart beat heavy against his chest, and he clenched his hands into a fist.

He stopped and turned when Beverly spoke. "Make sure he knows not to come near our Jaron again."

"And if the message I send gets me thrown in jail, you're bailing me out, right?"

Beverly had left his father in jail once or twice because she didn't approve of him drinking and getting into brawls at the bar. That had mostly been before Travis was born, but he'd heard the stories enough times to know he needed to have a way out.

"Of course. Now get that fool away from Jaron."

Travis nodded and left the room. It was as he passed the living room that he saw Jaron put the rug back in place, moving a table on top of it. He stopped in the hall, watching him through the open doorway.

Did Jaron feel safe on the farm? By God, he hoped so, but if he didn't, Travis would change that.

Travis rubbed at his chest. When had the ache started? He searched through his memory, trying to figure out which moment. That first day when Travis had walked them home and Jaron had met every advance with just enough distrust that it broke Travis' heart a little.

Travis had to earn it. He knew that but didn't know how to prepare himself for that uphill climb.

Jaron looked up from his task, meeting his gaze.

Travis wanted to tell him how safe and protected he was on the farm. He needed for Jaron to understand that no one would make him feel unwanted ever again.

Travis' dad had always said actions were louder than words. With that lesson planted in his brain, he walked down the hall toward the front door.

"Wait." Jaron's stocking feet barely made a sound as he trailed after Travis, but Travis could still feel his presence behind him. "Will you wait a damn minute?"

"I got stuff to do, so no." Travis pulled opened the front door and didn't wait for Jaron to respond. Jaron cursed right before the front door closed.

Travis searched for Leonard, the farm's supervisor. Leonard knew where to find Elmer.

Travis went into the cow barn first and found Leonard with Greg, teaching him about the drugs they sometimes administered, and the drugs' uses. They didn't have a lot, and what they did have most all farmers kept on hand.

"Where's Elmer?" Travis didn't wait for either of them to acknowledge his presence but got right down to business.

"Horse barn," Leonard said without stopping what he was doing.

Greg met his gaze, his eyes widening. He nudged Leonard with an elbow, getting his attention. Leonard looked at Greg before turning to Travis. "Got a temper just like your father used to. What bee got stuck in your bonnet this time, boy?"

Travis had been told that enough times in the past to recite it verbatim. "Might want to hire a new hand."

Leonard nodded, not seeming fazed by having to dole out extra work to the other hands or the hiring process. "Elmer doesn't fit in on this farm anyway. Not with any of us. You get what I'm saying, boy."

"Yep." Travis could read between the lines Leonard drew and knew enough to know the rest of the guys didn't just dislike the hate speech Elmer probably spewed, but they all protected each other as well. If one of them identified as anything other than straight, the others would protect him. And Elmer was the new guy amongst them. He'd have something to prove to the rest. "Guess this just saved us a conversation, didn't it?"

"Never pleasant to let the boss know the new guy sucks."

Travis turned and left them. He moved down the aisle, turning the corner exit at the main barn door which he knew was open.

He saw Jaron inside the barn, looking as if he didn't know if he wanted or should enter any farther. The second he saw Travis he closed the distance between them. His fists were on his hips and his elbows out. "What are you gonna do?"

Travis raised his eyebrows and pretended he didn't know what Jaron meant. "I'm going into the horse barn."

Jaron narrowed his eyes. "Don't play games with me."

"Go back into the house, Jaron."

"I'm on a break."

"Fine." Travis went to move around him, but Jaron stepped in his way. "Move. Please."

"Not until you tell me why you're so upset."

Travis had passed upset the second Jaron felt the need to use a broom-handle as a weapon. "I'm not upset. I'm pissed off. Now get out of my way so I can take care of business."

"What business?"

Travis sighed and decided to physically move Jaron himself. Jaron's throat moved when Travis grew closer. Whether in fear or something else, Travis couldn't tell. "Are you scared of me?" He had to know. He couldn't have taken it if Jaron said *yes*.

Jaron shook his head and dropped his arms from his sides, which gave Travis the opportunity he needed. Travis gripped Jaron's waist as gently as he could. "Good. I'd never hurt you."

"You're gonna. Just not in the way you mean." The whole time Jaron spoke, he trained his gaze on Travis' lips.

Travis shook his head. "Guess I have a lot to prove then, don't I?"

Jaron leaned in at the same time his mouth opened.

Travis wanted more than anything to kiss Jaron, but he was pissed enough still that the kiss would come off as aggressive and possessive. Something told Travis Jaron wouldn't appreciate either one of those two things. Instead, he did what he intended and lifted Jaron, turning them, so he had a clear path.

He let go and headed out of the door. "Don't follow me into the horse barn."

Jaron didn't say a word, but Travis heard his shoes on the concrete of the barn and then on the gravel when he stepped outside. Jaron stayed behind him the entire walk over to the horse barn.

"Don't follow me."

"Fuck you."

"Stop. I mean it." Travis turned at the door's entrance, ready to give him one final warning but was met with Jaron's middle finger. The gesture should have pissed him off even more, but somehow it had the exact opposite effect. "Why are you so hard-headed?"

"Why are *you* hot-headed?"

Travis smiled, his body relaxing as he lost most of his tension. "Well, that implies you knew I intended to beat the shit out of Elmer."

"You're not that hard to figure out." Jaron folded his arms over his chest. "You don't have to fight my battles."

"I'm not. I'm making the farm a nice place for all of us, you included."

"Then why'd you get so mad?"

Yeah, he wasn't about to answer that question. The answer made Jaron right about Travis fighting his battles and gave away his motivation when he wasn't ready for that yet.

It turned out he didn't have to answer because Elmer came out of the barn. He nodded to Travis by way of greeting. "Boss."

The look he gave Jaron set Travis' mind in a fog of anger all over again. Travis had never sucker-punched anyone, and he wouldn't start with Elmer. "Get your shit and get off my property."

Jaron's face turned a pretty shade of pink, and he took a step away as if backing up from the situation.

Elmer looked from Travis to Jaron. "I ain't workin' for someone who takes up with men like him anyway."

"Men like what?" Travis needed a reason. He took a step in Elmer's direction, balling his fists as he stalked him. "Say it. Just one fucking word is all I'll need."

Elmer's eyes widened, and he shook his head before practically running for the bunkhouse.

Travis took a deep breath, trying to calm himself. "Do me a favor and stay in the house until after he leaves. I'd feel better."

He felt a hand on his back. Just that one touch put out some of the fire. "Thank you."

"You don't have to thank me for doing the right thing."

"Some don't."

Travis turned to meet his gaze. "I do." He searched Jaron's gaze, although he didn't know what he wanted to find...peace-of-mind...acceptance. Jaron's expression was hard to read. "I'll drive you from now on, okay?"

Jaron nodded before kissing Travis on the cheek. He went back inside after, a pretty blush covering his cheeks as he left.

Travis took off his shoes at the door the second time he entered the house. He wouldn't get away with it again, not with the threat of Elmer gone.

He found his mother in the library reading a book in the sitting area. "You're not covered in manure, are you?"

Travis smiled and shut the library door behind him, not wanting Jaron to hear their conversation. "No, ma'am."

She set the book down on the table beside her when he sat next to her. "I trust Elmer is off the property."

"Yes, ma'am."

She patted his hand. "I'll make sure all the busybodies in this town know where we stand as far as all that goes."

"That's probably a good idea, considering."

"Considering you're in love with Jaron." Beverly wrapped her fingers around his hand, gently squeezing even as she smiled. "It's about time you found someone compatible."

"I don't know about love just yet. Or compatibility."

"I see the way you look at him."

Travis met his mother's gaze. "I don't know that I'm willing to act on the attraction. Running the farm keeps me busy, and Jaron has a kid. Not that his kid isn't the cutest, but I've never been serious about anyone."

"You always did like to have fun." She patted his hand again. "You haven't had a lot of that since your father passed away. Relationships can be a lot of fun. And Jaron strikes me as someone who will keep you on your toes."

He couldn't argue with her on that last part. "He's pretty much told me it would be a serious attempt at a relationship or nothing at all."

Beverly chuckled. "I'll just bet he did."

Travis stood and paced around the room. "It's not funny."

"Of course, you wouldn't think so." Beverly seemed to take mercy on him because she lost her smile. "Do you want some advice?"

"That's why I came in here."

"The sooner you admit to yourself that you're smitten with him, the better you'll feel."

Travis sighed.

"You've always been comfortable in your own skin and with the way you live your life. While that's a good thing, you never understood that not everyone is comfortable with you."

"Are you warning me about bigots, because it's a little too late for that talk."

"No. That talk isn't needed. This is Pickleville, after all." She waved away the conversation with a flick of her fingers. "I'm saying that perhaps Jaron doesn't have the same experiences as you do. He may not be as comfortable with himself as he lets on. I see the uncertainty with a lot of the decisions he makes. Bobby starting school so late in the year is a case in point."

Travis stopped and met her gaze. "You think he's scared he's going to mess up and ruin Bobby's life."

"Every good parent's worst fear is that they'll make big mistakes."

And with Bobby's mother dying the way she did, every decision Jaron made probably scared him.

Chapter Thirteen

♥

Jaron searched the closet in his room for his old board games and coming up empty. "Mom!"

He moved around a pair of binoculars he never remembered having. He certainly didn't remember ever using them, although he could think of a bedroom window he'd like to peek into. One glimpse of a naked Travis wasn't enough that was for sure. Maybe he could become a peeping tom. He'd probably excel at it.

"Mom!" An entire case of cassettes sat next to the binoculars, but still no board games.

He sighed and decided to find her.

Leaving his closet door open, he went to find his mother and saw Beth standing with her in the living room. "Hi."

"Want to go dancing? There will be a group of us." She had on a skirt that didn't make him think of her as a teacher. It was leather and small. The blouse she paired with it showed cleavage.

His mom stood next to her with a smile. "You have company."

"I don't have to go to school, right?" Bobby didn't avert his gaze from the movie he watched. He ate popcorn but got more on the couch than in his mouth.

Mom and Beth both chuckled, but it was Beth who answered. "Nope. I'm here to take your Papa out." She met Jaron's gaze. "I have it on good authority that you never leave the house, except for work."

Jaron narrowed his eyes at his mom, but he couldn't keep the smile off his face. "Tattletale."

"Go have fun with your friends." She walked over to the closet in the hallway and pulled down a board game he had played as a kid.

"Thanks, Mom."

"You need friends, Jaron." She touched his shoulder. "Have you even called Brian yet?"

Yeah, that wasn't a conversation he wanted to have because he didn't know what reception he'd get. He'd hurt Brian by leaving as much as he'd hurt his mom, although he understood the hurt came from a different place for each of them. Mom feared for his safety more than anything. As a parent himself, he understood her better since coming back. Brian had wanted a relationship, and Jaron had rejected him.

"You're right. I'll call him soon."

"Go out and have a good time."

"I'll try." Jaron practically ran to Beth and grabbed her hand, pulling her into his bedroom.

She looked around the room, taking in all his teenage angst. "Wow."

"I know. I'd change it, but I'm thinking of moving onto the Heath farm. Transportation to and from work would be less of an issue if I did."

She sat on the bed. "Not a bad idea. Bobby would love all the animals, I bet."

"I haven't been out in so long. I don't know that I have the right clothes anymore." Jaron smiled and pulled a shirt out of his closet, holding it up.

She shook her head. "Fully submersed yourself in Papa mode, huh?"

"Yeah, I guess. Honestly, Bobby's mom partied enough for both of us. One of us had to stay on the level."

"So you over-compensated for her. Makes sense."

Jaron held up a button-down shirt that he only wore one other time. "Yes. Didn't look at it that way, though."

She nodded. "Well, just know, from a teacher's point-of-view—"

"From my favorite teacher's point-of-view." Jaron smiled and put the shirt on the bed beside her.

She blushed. "Thank you. I always thought you were more mature than most of the others your age, although I'm only six years older than you so what do I know. I look at this room and realize how very wrong I was."

Jaron chuckled. "Shut up."

Beth pointed to a pair of black jeans. "Wear those."

Jaron pulled them from the hanger. "What were you about to say before I interrupted?"

"That having adult fun, whatever that means for you, from time to time would be good for you and Bobby. You're connecting with other adults, which you need, and Bobby sees how interactions with his peers are beneficial. Now enough about raising kids. You're doing a great job." She stood and handed him the shirt from the bed.

Jaron let Beth drive. He didn't want to take his mother's car and leave her without one if an emergency happened. When they pulled into the local bar's parking lot, Jaron grew a little nervous.

"Umm…I'll get my ass kicked here." The bar was the only local one for five miles. The neighboring town of Dalton had one. Jaron hadn't ever been in either one of them. He passed by them both going to and from some other place. The outside with its dark wood siding, and dimly lit parking lot hadn't changed much.

"A couple of years ago the bar changed owners."

Jaron nodded.

"Well, Royce bought up the bar a few years ago. He hired a manager and a bunch of bouncers. He told the manager he wanted the bar to be a safe place. Inclusive. I think he wanted a safe place to go after work. He's gay and everyone in town knows it. Some of the good ole boys used to cause him problems, but they learned their lesson really quick when all the businesses he owned wouldn't cater to them. He runs the auto shop in town too and owns the grocery store. His cousin owns the bar now."

"Well, cautious but hopeful, I guess."

Beth turned off the engine and put her keys in her purse. She still didn't get out of the car, though.

Jaron took off his seatbelt but waited for her to tell him whatever made her nervous. He didn't have to wait long.

"I'm in love with my best friend." Beth pointed to a car parked next to the building. "That's her car. Didn't expect her to be here. I purposefully didn't invite her. I bet Trina did. Nosy bitch."

Great. Why did Jaron always walk into drama? Why?

Jaron raised his eyebrows. "You haven't told your friend how you feel?"

"She knows something's wrong but doesn't know what. I've been avoiding her, which is why she came. She's never been one to like the silent treatment."

"You should just tell her."

"That takes courage I'm not sure I have."

Jaron patted her shoulder before opening the door. "Come on. Let's rip it off like a bandage." He got out, walked around the front of the car, opened her door, and held out his hand for her to take, wiggling his fingers when she hesitated. "Be brave."

Beth chuckled and let him pull her out of the car. The *thump* of the bass reached them across the parking lot. When they opened the front door, the music blared loud enough he could barely hear himself think.

Beth scanned the room. Her eyes landed on a table full of people to the left. She stiffened beside him but didn't hesitate in her steps.

"Hey, guys. This is Jaron." She made sure to keep him beside her, and they both sat down.

He noticed she stayed close, holding his hand, using him as a shield of sorts. Jaron let her and waved at the others with his free hand.

She didn't bother making introductions as the live band wailed on the guitar and beat hard on the drums, making talking impossible. He doubted the others heard what he said anyway.

The only other man at the table pointed to him and made a drinking gesture with his hand. The guy had his arm around a blonde woman, who had a ready smile.

Jaron nodded and pointed to the beer the man drank. He stood and kissed the blonde on the cheek before going to the bar.

A woman at the far corner of the table eyed Beth warily, which said more than anything she was the best friend. She had black hair that curled around her head and hung to her shoulders. She had on a button-down, purple shirt that made her dark skin tone stand out.

Beth actively avoided making eye contact.

Jaron sighed and decided to take matters into his own hands. He pointed to the woman and made a hand gesture that he hoped she understood to mean switch seats. She smiled and nodded, standing at the same time he did.

Beth watched them both as they moved around.

When he crossed paths with the best friend, he held out his hand and leaned forward. "I'm Jaron."

"Sherry. Thanks for switching with me."

"Of course." He hoped they both worked out whatever misunderstanding they had. Whatever their relationship status, they both seemed to want the other in their life in some capacity.

He sat down next to the blonde just as the guy came back, setting a glass of wine in front of Beth and a bottle of beer in front of Jaron.

"Thank you." Jaron had to yell it, but the guy nodded.

Beth narrowed her eyes at him, but he grinned, winking to let her know he didn't care if she didn't like it.

The blonde leaned into him. "I'm Trina, and this is my boyfriend, Gene."

"Jaron."

"I know. I graduated a couple of years before you, but I remember you from Spanish class."

Jaron smiled. "I thought you looked familiar."

The band ended their song and said something about taking a short break. Multiple conversations buzzed around them.

Two women who sat across from him introduced themselves. "I'm Amalia, and this is Raquel." Amalia made a gesture with her head. "Travis Heath has been eying you since you got here."

When did Travis get there? Jaron wanted to look around but didn't want to make it obvious. He leaned across the table. "Where?"

"In a booth right behind you."

Jaron took a deep breath and then turned. Sure enough, Travis sat in a booth beside Brad Flynn. Jaron had a moment of panic at seeing Brad but then he remembered how Travis had defended him. Travis' presence certainly helped stem the panic.

Travis had a bottle of water on the table in front of him. Their gazes met, and Jaron smiled, lifting a hand to wave. Travis smiled back and winked.

When Jaron turned to his group, Amalia and Raquel, both stared at him as if ready for a story. Jaron had no story to tell, and even if he did, he wouldn't tell it to people he barely knew.

"What's the deal?"

Jaron shrugged. "Deal about what?"

"Travis winked. And he looks like he wants to lick you like an ice cream cone."

Good thing Jaron hadn't taken a drink of his beer. He would have choked on it. "I doubt that."

"Me too," Trina spoke up from beside him. "He's not gay. I went out with him once."

"Just because Travis Heath went out with you in tenth grade doesn't mean he isn't gay," Beth said and then drank from her glass.

Sherry leaned into her until they were touching. Her hand was on Beth's back, and Jaron knew then that whatever friendship they had would blossom into something else. "He could be bisexual or have another preference he hasn't told anyone about."

Amalia's dark eyes sparkled. "Well, I get it. You're pretty, Jaron."

Jaron rolled his eyes, shaking his head. His face heated and he chuckled. "Thanks. I guess."

"Hell, I'm straight, and even I'd agree with that." Gene took a drink of his beer after he made that statement.

His face heated even more, which made everyone laugh.

Jaron felt a vibration in his pocket. He grabbed his phone and saw Travis' name in the text window. *Are they talking about me?*

No.

Liar. Jaron smiled at that.

Calling me pretty.

I agree.

Jaron rolled his eyes again and pocketed his phone.

Everyone at the table watched him. Before Jaron could respond, a waitress placed a drink next to his beer. "I didn't order that."

She nodded over to the bar. Shoving a napkin in his hand. "From the guy at the bar."

Jaron looked in the direction she indicated and saw more than one man sitting there with several people standing around in front of them. Everyone was talking and drinking, catching up on the weekly happenings around town. Most knew each other and were farmers or worked at the factory and wanted a drink to settle the week they just had. It took him a few seconds, but he'd have recognized Brian anywhere.

Brian had dark-rimmed glasses that seemed to bring out his dark eyes. He had filled out more, no longer a skinny kid, but a leanly muscled man. He wasn't big and bulky like Travis, but he clearly worked out. Everything else remained exactly as Jaron remembered.

Every regret about not staying in touch with Brian for those years flooded into his chest, making it ache. He clutched the napkin, fisting his fingers around it, even as he stood. He moved around people, an urgency building in his gut.

When he got to Brian, he didn't hesitate to hug. "I'm sorry I haven't called."

"That road goes both ways."

Jaron nodded and tightened his hold. "I really missed you, man."

Brian patted his back right before he pulled away. He slid from the stool. "Let's take this outside where we can talk a little better."

Jaron grabbed Brian's hand and pulled him out of the front door. He stopped under the building's overhead light and let Brian's hand go. "Sorry if the PDA was too much."

"It wasn't. Brad nearly shit kittens and Travis looked as if he wants to rip my head off. Other than that, it was fine." Brian took Jaron's hand again, lacing their fingers together. "I missed you too."

"Brad won't come out here and hurt us?"

Brian shook his head. "Not without getting kicked out of the bar for good. He knows that and as much as he drinks, it's a motivating factor."

When silence fell between them, Jaron cleared his throat. "We...um...why is this weird?"

Brian smiled and shrugged. "I know why I avoided you. Why did you avoid me?"

"Because I fell off the grid and shouldn't have. I'm a little ashamed of it." Jaron could tell by Brian's expression that he didn't expect the candidness. "Now you?"

"Because you fell off the grid and I didn't know if it was because you knew I used to be just a little in love with you."

Oh. Well...that was...unexpected. Jaron averted his gaze to the tufts of grass clinging to life around the concrete base of the building and stones scattered at the bottom of each tuft.

Brian squeezed his hand gently. "Relax. It's not a declaration. Just being honest since you were."

"I wish I had felt that way about you too. For the record."

"So are we done giving each other the silent treatment?"

Jaron laughed and went in for another hug.

Brian returned the hug. "Is that a dildo in your pocket or are you just happy to see me."

"What?" It took him a moment to figure out what Brian meant, but when he did, he laughed. He pulled his phone out if his pocket and waved it at Brian. When he saw Travis' name, he didn't bother answering but put it back in his pocket.

"You don't have to answer it?"

Jaron shook his head. "No. It's not about Bobby."

"Bobby?"

"My son." Jaron pulled out his wallet and opened it, showing Brian a picture of Bobby.

Brian took his wallet and studied the picture. "You have a kid?"

"Yeah. He's five and in Beth's class at the elementary school." Jaron leaned in until their foreheads touched. He pointed to Bobby in the photograph. "That was at the beach last summer. We made the castle together. Bobby's mom stayed sober enough to come with us. That's her there." He had other pictures of Tracy, but none were as recent as the beach photo. Her eyes were clear in that one as well, which was why he liked it.

"Your son looks like her."

"Yes." Same blonde hair and blue eyes. "He does. He'll probably be tall like she was too, I think."

"What happened?"

Jaron didn't want to talk about Tracy. Not when Beth had asked him out so he could have fun. "How about we talk about it later?"

"Let's go inside and dance or something."

Jaron nodded, putting his wallet back in his pocket. "By the way, what drink did you buy me?"

"Jack and coke." Brian slung his arm over Jaron's shoulder, and they walked back into the bar together. "I didn't know what you drank."

"Never drank whiskey in my life." He'd only ever had a beer and had gotten drunk once. Once had been enough.

Chapter Fourteen

B eth and her friends were still discussing Travis when Jaron made
it back to the table. Jaron sat down, pulling Brian into the seat
next to him. "This is Brian." He went through everyone around the
table, pointing at each person, surprising himself that he remembered
their names.

"So Brian, what do you do for a living?" Of everyone in their group,
Amalia was the first one who would engage in conversation.

The band started up again, and no one could talk anymore, which
saved Brian from going into his life story.

Jaron felt his phone vibrate insistently once again. Travis had texted
twice. The first one read, *So?* The second held a bit of bite in every
word. *Where the fuck did you go? Are you all right?*

Jaron rolled his eyes. *I'm fine.*

It's about fucking time.

What?

Did Brian touch you?

What r u talking about? He would never hurt me.

I meant did you let him touch you in a sexual way.

That's it. *None of your business.*

It took Travis a full five minutes to respond.

All the while Jaron fumed and tried not to look Travis' way when the need for it pulled at his gut.

U r right. I'm being an asshole.

Jaron refused to respond.

Please.

Leave me alone. What a jerk. *We're not dating. Remember?*

Do you have a thing for Brian? Jaron put his phone into his pocket without responding.

It vibrated a couple of times, but he ignored it.

Beth stood and pulled Sherry to a doorway at the back of the bar. Jaron watched them with a satisfied smile. At least someone's night had gone in the right direction.

His phone vibrated again.

Trina must have finally talked Gene into dancing because they joined the few others when the band played a slow song.

A warm presence slid behind him and then Travis' breath fanned across his cheek. "I need to talk to you."

When Jaron turned, Travis moved just enough for their gazes to meet. Travis held out his hand, wanting Jaron to take it. Jaron shook his head and turned back to the other three occupants at the table.

Travis sat in the chair Trina had vacated, facing him. He took Jaron's hand right before pleading with his eyes.

Damn it. Why the hell did that look have to work on him?

Jaron sighed and nodded. Travis pulled him out of his chair and out of the bar.

It seemed like everyone watched them leave.

When they were outside and into the parking lot, Jaron thought they'd have whatever conversation Travis needed to have out in the open, but Travis pulled Jaron over to his truck.

"Did you meet Brian here?" Travis had Jaron against the side of the truck, penning him in before Jaron could protest, mostly because Travis' questions pissed him off. Travis angered him more than anyone else on the planet. Jaron didn't want to analyze the reason why. Instead, he focused on Travis' questions.

"None of your business."

"You are my business, Jaron."

"No, I'm not. I'm not one of your little weekend fucks, so stop treating me like I am."

"I know you're not."

"I doubt you even know what you're doing right now."

"For the first time in my life, I know exactly what I'm doing." Travis' gaze went right to Jaron's lips.

Jaron knew what Travis intended but couldn't let it happen. If he did, he would fall hard, and in the end, the fall would hurt. He put a hand over Travis' mouth. "You know my terms."

Travis nodded and removed Jaron's hand, holding it to his chest. "I don't want casual or anyone else. And I need you to tell me the same thing because I'm a possessive asshole. I'm sorry. I know that makes you mad, but I can't help the jealousy."

"Brian's my best friend from high school. Haven't seen him since I've been back. Friends is all, though. And no, I didn't meet him here. It's a small town with one bar. Just ran into each other."

"So you're saying yes?"

Jaron smiled. "I'm saying yes."

Travis looked at Jaron's lips right before he kissed him. When their lips came together, the kiss was tentative, as if Travis feared scaring Jaron or injuring him somehow. Maybe he just feared rejection.

Travis cupped Jaron's cheek and tilted his head to get a better angle. That started a slow ride to dominance.

Jaron let Travis take what he wanted. He let him turn the kiss from a hot coal to a burning flame one lick at a time. He wrapped his arms around Travis' shoulders and pulled him closer until Travis' body was flush against his. When he felt Travis' hard length against his abdomen, he forgot everything. Every thought vanished until all he knew was their physical connection. And if he felt that way with clothes on, he'd lose every brain cell he had when they finally got naked.

Travis pulled away first. He rested his forehead against Jaron's, taking the time to catch his breath.

"Why'd you stop?"

"Because if I don't, our first time will be in my truck. I can romance you better than that."

Jaron smiled and closed his eyes. "After that kiss, I don't know if you'll have to try very hard."

Travis chuckled.

"Think they'll come up for air soon?" Brian's voice might as well have been a bucket of ice water. It had the same effect.

Jaron shook and tried to push Travis away when he saw Jackson Bartlett and Brad Flynn standing in the parking lot just feet away from Brian, Beth and their little group.

Travis tightened his hold, angling them so no one saw Jaron.

All of the bullying he went through in high school flashed through his mind. Some deeds had etched themselves under the skin, festering at all the wrong moments. It didn't matter how many years had passed or the strides Jaron had taken to put all that behind him when his childhood bullies stood feet away.

Jackson had raised eyebrows but otherwise didn't seemed fazed. Brad had been the one who scared Jaron the most and always had. Time and distance hadn't changed that.

"Show's over." Travis ran a hand down Jaron's arm and kissed his temple. "I'll never let anyone hurt you. You're safe."

His attempt at soothing Jaron worked. He relaxed, and the urge to run left.

"I didn't know you were a faggot, Heath," Brad said. Jaron would never forget his harsh voice.

Jaron held his breath, shaking again. When he felt Travis stiffen against him, his focus changed. "Don't let him get to you." Looking over his shoulder at the others standing around, he implored one of them to help him calm the situation. Everyone's gaze was on Brad.

"Look at that. The little fag turned Heath." Brad's laughter followed.

Travis turned and went after Brad like a bullet.

Brad's head whipped back. He had blood on his lip. Some of it coated his teeth. When he returned the punch, Travis took it without stopping.

Travis punched Brad in the stomach and didn't wait for him to recover before knocking him backward with another fist to the face.

Brad's brawn made up for the couple of inches Travis had on him. He knew how to use all the muscle to his advantage too. When he came at Travis, he didn't hold anything back.

The only difference between Travis and Brad was that Travis didn't seem to feel a thing. He went after Brad like a pissed-off bull, giving him blow after blow.

"Travis!" Jaron yelled and finally moved off the truck when he realized Travis wouldn't stop. He tugged on Travis' arm, trying to pull him away, but he only succeeded in getting jerked around with every punch.

Jackson sighed and cursed, shaking his head before getting in between them. "Let it rest!"

When Jackson pushed Brad back, he stayed back, so he turned to Travis, holding him in place with his hands on his chest. Travis didn't quit. He tried to push past Jackson at every turn. "Don't come near him. You understand me."

"Calm down."

"Fuck you."

"You'll hurt Jaron." Jackson nodded to Jaron's hand on Travis' arm. "You'll elbow him on accident if you don't stop."

Travis looked at Jaron's hand. His expression softened by the time their gazes met. Jaron pulled gently on his arm until Travis came to him. Travis wrapped him up in a hug, and it was only then that Jaron realized he still shook.

"Let me take you home."

Jaron nodded. "Yeah, I've had enough excitement for one night."

Travis put him in the passenger seat of his truck and closed the door.

Chapter Fifteen

J aron wrung his hands as Travis parked his truck in Gloria's driveway but didn't shut off the engine. Tension hung in the air, pulling tighter the longer they sat there, waiting for the other to speak. Or maybe Travis waited for Jaron to get out of the truck. Maybe dating was off the table since Travis had seen just how difficult dating a man was in Pickleville. God, Jaron didn't know.

Jaron sighed and took off his seatbelt. When he reached for the door handle, Travis stopped him with a hand on his arm. Jaron looked at that hand, watching as Travis rubbed circles around the shirt fabric with his thumb. When he met Travis' gaze, he knew right away he pegged the tension wrong.

"I'm sorry I scared you."

Oh God, there went Jaron's heart. The tension disappeared, and Jaron slid across the seat, getting as close to Travis as he could. The center console stopped him from moving in even further.

Jaron cupped Travis' cheek. "I thought you were gonna kill him."

"As long as you're not scared of me."

"No. I'm not."

"I wouldn't have. Just wanted to make sure he knew not to come near you." Travis released his arm and slid his hand around Jaron's waist. "That wasn't the first time Brad's pissed me off. He's an asshole when he drinks sometimes, and he drinks a lot. He has family issues and uses alcohol to forget. Just want him to remember, even when he's shitfaced, what will happen if he comes near you again."

"You know him pretty well, huh?"

"I knew we'd have issues and I know we still will."

"I hope you don't fight again." Jaron ran his thumb over the bruise just starting to bloom below Travis' right eye. A bloody cut ran across the top of the bruise, but Jaron didn't touch it. "Come inside and let me clean you up."

Travis nodded and smiled. He took Jaron's hand, pulling it away from his cheek and held onto it briefly before letting him go again. He shut off the engine and pocketed his keys before getting out of the truck.

Jaron followed suit, taking Travis' hand in his own. It took him a second to get the door's lock open. The whole time he worked to open it, Travis stood behind him with his hands around Jaron's waist.

Their body heat mingled. Jaron leaned against Travis with his hand around the doorknob. "You make me feel safe." He hadn't felt safe since Tracy's death. Even moving to Pickleville hadn't helped that because Pickleville had never truly been safe. The situations with Elmer and Brad drove that home, but he had more allies than bullies. "It's unexpected."

Travis kissed him on his cheek. "I have your back. You can count on that."

Jaron turned the knob and led Travis over to the kitchen table. He pushed Travis down into one of the chairs. "I'll be right back." He whispered the words, not wanting to wake up Gloria or Bobby.

He checked on Bobby first. Bobby was a little lump under the covers, his blond hair the only thing Jaron saw. He didn't want to wake him up, so he pulled the door closed, leaving it open a crack.

He gathered what he needed from the bathroom and took it back into the kitchen. He placed it on the table beside Travis before putting some rubbing alcohol on a cotton ball. "This will burn. Sorry. It's all we had."

Travis let Jaron tilt his head to the side. "Won't hurt as bad as Brad's punch."

Jaron smiled. "No. Probably not." He bent down, dabbing at the cut with the soaked cotton ball.

Travis hissed and jerked back.

Jaron blew on it as he dabbed, trying to relieve the sting. "Just a little more and then we're done." He didn't pay attention to any other part of Travis but the cut. He threw away the cotton ball before coming back to him.

Travis wrapped an arm around Jaron's waist and reeled him in like a big fish.

Jaron smiled and straddled Travis' lap, knowing that's what he wanted. He grabbed the antibiotic ointment and put some on the tip of his fingers before applying it to the cut.

Travis jerked again but otherwise didn't make a move or protest.

When he finished, he wiped his fingers on the washcloths he had brought out with everything else and tried to stand, but Travis held him in place. He put the washcloth back on the table and smiled, meeting Travis' gaze. "I need to get you some ice for the swelling."

"It'll keep." Travis looked at him as if he were the only other person in the world. His whole face softened, and his eyes sparkled with something that went beyond lust. Travis was every romantic movie ever made.

Jaron couldn't help the heat from creeping into his face. He couldn't meet Travis' gaze.

Travis tilted Jaron's chin up when he averted his gaze. "What?"

Jaron smiled. "You."

"What did I do?"

"Let's just say, I completely understand why so many girls in our class drooled over you."

"Meaning."

"Meaning you're hard to resist, sir."

"That's funny. I was thinking the same thing about you."

Jaron leaned forward and kissed Travis, first on his bruise before moving to his lips. He kept the kiss gentle and didn't try to make demands. The kiss was meant to soothe some of the tension building between them. He wanted to take the edge off the burn. Nothing more. All the kiss did was fan the flame.

Travis worked his tongue around the rim of Jaron's lips, opening him up.

Jaron allowed him access. Whether Travis broke his heart or not was irrelevant. He waved the white flag and became a prisoner to whatever came next. Breaking away from the kiss, he was a little breathless, and a lot hard. "You are very good at kissing."

Travis smiled. "So are you." He pulled Jaron closer until their chests connected. Pressing his cheek against Jaron's, he took a deep breath, taking in Jaron's scent as if he needed to memorize it.

It wasn't until his mom entered the kitchen that either of them moved.

Jaron sat up and moved off Travis' lap even as he watched her get a cup from the cabinet and filled it with tap water. She drank from it and then put it on the counter beside her.

His mom turned and leaned against the counter, looking from Jaron to Travis and back again. She gave him the mom glare right before she spoke. "I expected you home later than this. You don't intend to have sex in my house, do you?"

Oh, God. If the floor opened and swallowed him whole, he would count it as a blessing. "No. I brought him inside to clean up his face."

Mom came off the counter and tilted Travis' face up to get a better look at the cut. "What happened?"

"Got into a fight, Ms. McAllister." Travis let her search his wound, and when she poked at the swelling around his cheekbone, he let her do that too.

"Get a freezer bag and fill it with ice, Jaron. Then grab a clean cloth from the bathroom."

Jaron smiled and obeyed her, getting a plastic bag from the drawer.

"Does you two snuggling up on each other have anything to do with the fight?"

"Yes, ma'am." Travis' politeness was cute.

Jaron put ice in the bag.

Mom focused on Travis' gaze. "You defended my son?"

"Yes, ma'am."

She smiled. "I hoped you kicked the other guy's ass."

"If I'm honest, ma'am, Brad's a better fighter. He didn't try that hard."

"You sent a message. That's the important thing."

"I agree."

Mom held out her hand for the ice pack, and Jaron handed it to her. She placed it on Travis' cheek and held it there. "Go get that cloth, Jaron."

Jaron shook his head but walked out of the room. He had just rounded the corner when he heard his mom speak again. "My Jaron has a good head on his shoulders and doesn't need you derailing him. If you're not serious about him, then you need to head out the door right now."

"My intentions are honorable."

"Then you can spend the night in Bobby's room." His mom had never said anything like that about him before. She certainly hadn't given anyone the protective parent talk.

Jaron sucked in a breath, his hand going to his chest when the ache set in. He hadn't been sure he made the right move when he came back home, not until he heard his mother's side of the conversation.

Chapter Sixteen

T he bed mattress bounced, waking Travis just enough to realized
he hadn't moved. Not even one finger, not to mention enough
to make the bed shift beneath him. Morning breath fanned across his
face. He tried to move away from it, not liking the smell very much.
No matter how far back he moved his head, the breath remained.

He popped one eye open, which turned out to be a mistake because
big blue eyes and a sweet face lay inches from him, sharing the pillow
he used. He jerked, and his breath caught.

His brain woke up enough, and his body settled.

The last time he'd woken up with a start had been when he slept
over at his mother's house after Maggie had her baby. He had been too
tired to walk the distance to his house, so he'd slept in his old room.
God only knew how long that pile of laundry had been lying there. It
had probably accumulated when he built the cabin and he'd finished
months ago. Jaron tripping got the ball rolling as far as cleaning up.
Much needed.

"You're a lot like your dad. Anyone ever tell you that?" Travis smiled
and rolled to his back. His cheek throbbed where Brad had punched
him. He raised his hands to look at his knuckles and found they
weren't that bruised. Lucky break.

"Why are you sleeping in my bed?" Bobby asked. Leave it to a kid to get right down to the bones of it all.

"Because I needed a place to sleep." And he hadn't wanted to leave Jaron alone after the fight. Travis had a gut feeling Brad would try something else, and he wanted to keep Jaron close just in case.

"I always sleep with Papa. He likes to snuggle. You can sleep with him too."

Travis smiled. He would've loved nothing more than to curl up next to Jaron, but they had a few things to discuss before they got to that stage. A talk about the little angel in the bed with him hit the number one priority spot. He wouldn't go against whatever rules Jaron had about Bobby seeing them in the same bed together.

Bobby did look like an angel too, quite literally, except without the wings and halo, but Travis could imagine both. He had an innocent quality that kicked Travis' protective instinct into high gear. Bobby should keep that quality about him for as long as possible.

Bobby scrambled off the bed, grabbing Travis' hand and tugging. "Cereal."

Travis regretted sitting up. He groaned and rolled his head around on his neck to work out the worst of the kinks.

Yep, Brad had kicked his ass last night. Every single bruise and muscle ached.

Bobby tugged until Travis stood, not cutting him any slack. When they got to the kitchen, Bobby let him go and sat in the same kitchen chair Travis had sat in last night. "I want the chocolate kind."

"Chocolate, huh?" Travis proceeded to open cabinets until he came to the one with three boxes of cereal lining the shelves. Travis grabbed a brown box with a bird on the front and set it in the center of the table before rummaging around for a spoon and bowl. After pouring the cereal and then milk, he placed the bowl in front of Bobby and sat at the table with him.

"I'm in kindergarten," Bobby spoke around a spoonful of breakfast.

"Do you like it?"

Bobby just shrugged. "I like Mackenzie. He's our class hamster."

"So you like animals?"

Bobby nodded. "And I like Papa."

Travis smiled. "What kind of animal is he?" He should get up and make coffee, but the conversation with Bobby entertained him enough that he didn't want to interrupt the flow.

Bobby giggled. "He's not an animal, silly."

"I like your Papa too."

"You do?"

"Yep. Is that okay with you?"

"I guess so. That means you're gonna be nice to him. Cuz if you like someone, then you're nice. If you don't like someone, then you're mean." Simplistic but true for a five-year-old.

"Do you like puppies?"

Bobby's blue eyes got bigger if that was possible, and a smile lit up his face. He nodded. "Papa said he wants me to buy him a dog when I get rich. He's gonna name it Booger. But it's gotta be green." Bobby's little frown over the last statement had Travis chuckling.

"Dogs aren't green."

"I know. But I don't think Papa knows that."

"How are you gonna tell him?"

Bobby thought about that for a minute. His little face scrunched up in concentration. "Maybe if he saw one. Do you have puppies?" Bobby's blue eyes lit up with intelligent mischief that surprised Travis but probably shouldn't have.

"It just so happens that I do."

"Really?"

"Mm-hmm. You want to come to my house and play with them? If your papa says it's okay."

Bobby looked at something over Travis' shoulder. "Is it?"

Travis turned to see the most beautiful person he had ever seen. A good night's sleep had disheveled his dark curls, and his eyes still reflected sleep. Travis would give anything to wake up next to that every morning.

Jaron smiled at him and said, "Good morning." He squeezed Travis' shoulder and gave him a peck on the cheek as he walked past to get to the coffee maker. "Good morning, snuggle bear."

"Can we see the puppies?" The kid had a one-track mind.

"I suppose." Jaron met Travis' gaze. A smile touched his lips. "I saw the mother dog had them in the yard the other day and wanted to bring Bobby by sometime. To see the horses and cows too. That is if you don't have other plans."

"Nothing pressing." He wanted a shower and to change out of last night's clothes. Other than that, he could leave the farm in Leonard's capable hands for one day.

Jaron fiddled with the coffee maker, not turning until he had coffee brewing. When he did, he leaned against the counter, meeting Travis' gaze. One corner of Jaron's mouth went up, and he shrugged. "Date at your house with my kid and a bunch of dogs?"

"I'm in." Was he over his head? Probably but he'd happily drown if it meant he'd get more time with Jaron and Bobby.

They took a booster seat from Gloria's car and put it in Travis' truck.

Travis noticed the domesticity of the seat and liked it. A baggie of cereal lay in the seat beside it, and a bottle of juice sat in the little cup holder thing attached.

Jaron had packed a change of clothes for Bobby *just in case* he spilled or got dirty, which seemed like a very parental move and not something Travis would have thought to do.

None of it bothered Travis the way he expected. At least not in a way that would've made him turn the truck around.

Travis looked at Jaron in the passenger's seat as he pointed out the cattle in the field on the left.

No, he wanted Jaron and Bobby in his life. Every little representation of family hit him in the chest hard enough it stole his breath. He could only think about his father and what he would think about the little boy strapped into the car seat practically bouncing out of it when he saw a few horses in the next field over.

"Can I ride a horse?"

Jaron said no at the same time Travis said yes.

"Those horses belong to the neighbor. But if you want to ride, you'll have to get to know some of the horses on my farm first." Travis met Jaron's gaze for a moment before turning back to the road again. "How's that for a compromise?"

Jaron shook his head, but he smiled, rolling his eyes. "How old were you when you learned?"

"Four or five, I guess. My dad taught me." And Travis would pass on that knowledge to Bobby if Jaron would let him. "I'll let him ride with me the first few dozen times. And we'll ride one of the beginner horses. Deal?"

"I guess." Jaron sighed.

Travis turned into his driveway. "I'll introduce you to some of the horses later. How's that sound, little man?"

Bobby grinned and nodded.

Lila already had her puppies playing in the side yard under the oak tree. The poor girl looked tired but happy to lie in the shade.

He shut off the truck's engine, laid his keys on the floor, and walked around to get Bobby out of the backseat. As soon as he put Bobby on his feet, he ran to the puppies.

Jaron was already out of the truck by then. He put his arm around Travis' waist and met his gaze. "I know I'm over-protective about the horse-riding thing."

"Really? I didn't notice." Travis pulled Jaron close and kissed the top of his head, smiling through the teasing.

Jaron turned, so they faced each other. "I do trust you with Bobby's safety."

"But he's still your baby." Travis cupped his cheek right before he kissed Jaron. The press of lips wasn't designed to do anything, but comfort. It seemed to work because Jaron pressed his cheek to Travis' chest. "I get it. And it never crossed my mind that you didn't trust me so stop worrying."

"I feel like I'm going to say or do something."

Travis watched Bobby as he sat on the ground.

When five puppies surrounded him, assaulting him with licks and playful yips, Bobby giggled.

"What do you mean?"

Jaron sighed and pulled back. He turned and saw Bobby. He smiled, but it didn't quite reach his eyes. "I'm complicating things, and I'm about to make it even more complicated."

Travis shook his head and ran his hand across his forehead. "Why don't we go into the main house and get something to eat. We'll still be able to keep an eye on Bobby and the pups if we wrangle them into the backyard. We can discuss whatever you need to while we eat."

Jaron chuckled, but nodded. "You make them seem like cattle."

"There's a reason why Lila's lying there looking grateful to have Bobby over for a playdate."

They ate at the picnic table because the sun felt nice, and they could keep an eye on Bobby better. Travis made a simple omelet with a few veggies, bacon, and cheese, and they had coffee with it. Well, Travis had coffee. Jaron had a cup full of sugar mostly. Bobby had eaten cereal earlier and didn't seem to care about food when he had the puppies as playmates.

"What's on your mind, baby?" Wanting to get whatever needed to be said out of the way.

Jaron wiggled around on the seat. "We've only just started dating. I know that. But I already feel like it's serious."

"It feels new, but also like we've been playing around each other forever." The contrasting feeling left him a bit uneasy as well, but not in a bad way. The tension between them drew them together until all Travis wanted was to make love right there in his mother's backyard. They couldn't though. The push and pull of it intrigued him enough that he was content just to let things happen. "Sexual tension."

Jaron tilted his head to the side and pursed his lips as if contemplating that. "I guess you're right. Been a long time. I guess I didn't recognize it."

Travis grunted around a bite of food, swallowing it down. He smiled. "There's a remedy for that."

Jaron chuckled and pointed his fork at Travis. "We need to talk first."

"Yeah, I know. And I know you might trust me with Bobby, but you don't trust me with you just yet. You're guarded."

"True. And I'm sorry."

"Don't be. I'm not proud of it, but I've earned my reputation. I don't go out much anymore. Since Dad died, the farm has taken up a lot of my attention. Last night was the first night I've been out in over a year."

Jaron shook his head. "You were out the other night. Your mom mentioned you'd had a late night."

Travis had to think back. If it were spring, he'd have a lot of late nights helping the spring babies come into the world. Since fall, he'd only had one. "You're talking about the night Maggie had her baby."

Jaron shrugged.

"I helped her deliver. That's why I slept at mom's house."

"Wait, you don't live here?" Jaron's mouth went slack, and his eyes rounded.

Travis chuckled and shook his head. He pointed in the direction of his house. "See that path through the forest."

Jaron had to lean forward to see it as part of the house blocked his view but only just. He moved his plate to the side when he realized he'd get food all over his pants if he didn't.

An inch or two separated them. Travis studied him for the longest time, taking in the slight stubble across his cheek and the way his skin still looked smooth to the touch despite it. "The two-track?"

"Yeah. My house is a short walk down it. We passed my driveway on the way here."

"Oh." When Jaron turned to meet his gaze, their lips almost touched.

Travis took advantage, closing the distance. He didn't make demands with the kiss. Jaron didn't trust him enough to understand what Travis wanted from him. As much as he wanted to believe actions spoke louder than words, Travis knew he had a little more talking to do.

The kiss brought as much heat as those last night did. Every time they connected, it tightened the tension. They'd both go up in flames soon if they didn't do something about it.

When Jaron pulled away, he hovered an inch from Travis, studying him. The picnic table bounced when he sat down, even on Travis' side of the table. His eyes were still glassy when he blinked.

Travis knew the feeling. "It's never been like that for me either." Not one fucking time and a part of him didn't know what to do about that, except for the obvious.

Before Jaron could comment, Bobby came racing over holding a brown and white puppy in his arms, and four others were bouncing around behind him.

"He's cute." Travis smiled.

Jaron smiled. "Yeah, and so is the dog. Together they could rule the world."

Travis snorted out a laugh and would have commented on the dramatic way Jaron said that, but Bobby held up the puppy as if asking Jaron to inspect it.

"Papa, can I keep him?"

Jaron looked to Travis for help. "Bobby, why don't you go in and get something to drink? No soda, though."

"After you talk to Travis, will you let me have a puppy?"

Travis burst out laughing. "Smart kid."

Bobby put the puppy down and then went into the house through the back door. The little dogs didn't understand that they couldn't follow him. Bobby stopped with one hand on the knob and waved a finger at the puppies. "No, no."

Four of the five sat down, cocking their heads to the side, trying to figure out Bobby's meaning. The fifth one was the maverick and stole Travis' heart when he plowed through the crack in the door. Bobby sighed and picked him up, putting him back outside. "I said no, little man."

Bobby smiled at Travis as if wanting his approval.

"You make a great puppy wrangler." Travis could tell Bobby wanted his approval because he beamed as he shut the door behind him.

Travis could hear him call out his mom's name even through the door.

"Are you gonna let him have a puppy?"

"That depends on how weirded out you'd be if I moved in here. Bev offered when I first started, but I wanted to wait. Seeing Bobby here makes me think this is the right place for us."

It made sense that Mom would want someone with her every day, and she'd had a live-in housekeeper before. She didn't complain of loneliness, but Travis worried. That wasn't what gave him pause.

Travis' silence must have made Jaron fearful of rejection because his shoulders came up to his ears and he spoke again. "Starting this week, I'd have him get off the bus here anyway. I thought to start him on that routine for a couple of weeks and then maybe spend the night a couple of times a week. Gradually leave our stuff here. That way I'm not dragging him away from another home again."

"Might as well move into my house. It's where you're gonna end up in a few months anyway. It'll save you another move." Travis pushed Jaron's plate back into place. "Finish eating."

Jaron didn't even bother picking up his fork. Instead, he stared at Travis as if he'd grown another eyeball in the center of his forehead. He opened his mouth to speak, but then closed it again. He shook his head. "I can't move in with you. It's way too soon, and you know it."

Travis shrugged. "I'm just giving it to you straight, Jaron."

"Meaning."

"My intentions are clear. I'm just saving you some time." Travis had never seen Jaron so flabbergasted. As cute as it was, he took pity on him. "I'll move back in with Mom and rent you my house until we're ready for that step. We can draw up a renter's agreement if it makes you feel better. I'll even make the rent reasonable but fair. Deal?"

Jaron huffed and put his elbows on the table. "I don't know."

Travis chuckled and stood, coming around the table. The puppies barreled toward him when he moved, and he had to step over them as he walked. He straddled the bench, crowding Jaron with his legs. He wrapped his arms around Jaron's waist and pulled him closer, kissing just below his ear. "I'll support whatever decision you make. Gloria's house, Mom's, or renting mine. You got options."

"I want Bobby on the farm. He'd thrive here."

"I'd teach him everything about the farm if he wants to learn." Travis kissed Jaron farther down on his neck.

Jaron shut his eyes and tilted his head to the side, giving Travis better access. "And if we don't work out?"

Travis pulled back and turned Jaron until their gazes met. "That won't have anything to do with Bobby. He'd still get my attention. If you move to the farm, you'll both always have a home here. It's how this family works. Understand?"

Jaron nodded. "Yes, I understand."

"Good." Travis tilted Jaron's head back and placed a wet kiss complete with just a hint of tongue on the place where Jaron's neck and shoulder met. "So, are you gonna let him have a puppy?"

Chapter Seventeen

In under a week, things around the farm changed. The weather called for long-sleeves and a jacket every time they stepped outside. Gone were the days when T-shirts offered the most comfort. Harvesting the last of the crops and storing them properly took up most of the time. But it wasn't the weather or the crops that changed. Travis felt different. The empty spaces he didn't even know he had, filled up, grounding him to the earth in a way working it hadn't even done. His purpose had changed.

His purpose walked out of the front door of the house with an empty half-bushel in his hands and one of the puppies following him. The little dog's ears flopped around as he ran to catch up.

Travis smiled when Jaron stopped and turned, scooping the puppy into his arms before setting off again.

Travis turned to Greg. "I'll be right back."

Greg grinned. "Just remember that I'm still an impressionable child so maybe accost him around the side of the barn where I can't see."

Travis shook his head. "That was the plan."

Greg made a face. They had an older brother, younger brother thing going on most days. Travis and Jaron's make out sections grossed Greg out. Travis would have laughed and poked fun if he wasn't a man on a mission.

He jogged to catch up with Jaron, and by the time he did, Jaron had put the dog down again. Travis pushed Jaron up against the barn, pinning him in place.

Jaron sucked in a breath and stiffened but relaxed once he figured out who had him. He let the half-bushel fall from his hand and wrapped his arms around Travis' neck, grinning. "I have stuff to do before Bobby gets off the bus."

"What is more important than making out with me?" Travis ran the back of his finger down Jaron's cheek.

"Cauliflower." Jaron's eyes sparkled with humor even as his focus never left Travis' lips.

He chuckled. "You're always so sensible."

"And your mind is always on one thing." If that bothered Jaron, he didn't show it.

"Are you complaining?"

"Not even a little." Jaron leaned in until his lips were inches from Travis. "In fact, I want to know how long it's gonna be before you take me to the hayloft. You're slacking, farm boy."

Travis closed the distance between them, stealing a quick kiss. "The first time we make love won't be in the hayloft."

Jaron shrugged. "The second time works for me."

Travis chuckled again. "Compromise. I like it."

As soon as Jaron's lips touched his again, the puppy grabbed onto his pant leg, playing tug of war with him. He tried to heat up the kiss, but the pull on his pant leg killed the moment. He chuckled and pressed their foreheads together. "Spend the night with me tonight."

"What about Bobby?"

"Well, I want him to spend the night too, of course." He wouldn't mind spending the weekend giving Bobby riding lessons. He planned on getting started that evening sometime after Bobby got off the bus.

"I think he's ready for a sleepover. God knows I am."

"I got a room ready for him at the house. Mom kept all my horse stuff, books included. He has a bookshelf we can help fill for him and a bin of toys. A few are new." Travis pulled his head back, meeting Jaron's gaze. "The house is almost ready for you guys. Gotta move some clothes out, and it's all yours."

Jaron tightened his hold around Travis' shoulders, going up on his tiptoes, dragging Travis down until their cheeks pressed together. "You're really great. Do you know that?"

Travis slid his arms around Jaron. "I don't know. My motivation is purely selfish. I want you and Bobby. As close as possible for as long as possible."

Tires crunched on gravel, alerting Travis to a visitor. A flash of a shiny white truck out of the corner of his eyes told him it was probably Jackson. He had a horse in Travis' barn that he wanted to keep secret from his father. Jackson hadn't checked on it in a while and was overdue.

Jaron didn't seem to notice the sound. Either that or he didn't care because he didn't end the hug. It wasn't until footsteps sounded on the gravel that Jaron made a move and that was to stiffen.

Travis rubbed circles on Jaron's back. "It's just Jackson."

Jackson nodded as he came around the corner of the barn. "Just came to check on my horse and to see how much I owe you for keeping it."

"I didn't work out the math. I will by Sunday, though."

Jackson took in the puppy at their feet and bent down, calling the little dog. The puppy ran to him. It's tongue lolled and ears flapped the whole way. Jackson petted him but didn't take his eyes off them.

Jaron loosened his hold, his body relaxing by slow degrees. He turned Jackson's way but didn't say anything.

Jackson smiled and held up a hand. "Nice meeting the person who has Travis all tied up in knots. Well, re-meeting, I suppose."

And just like that the rest of Jaron's misgivings disappeared. He met Travis' gaze. "I have you tied in knots?"

Jaron might have asked Travis, but Jackson answered. "Oh yeah. He wouldn't have gone after Brad if you didn't."

Travis narrowed his eyes. It was all for show, and Jackson must have known it because he chuckled.

Jaron picked up the half-bushel before kissing Travis one last time. He turned toward the back garden. "Come on, dog." He tapped his hand on his leg, using the sound to get the pup's attention.

Travis kept his eyes on his ass as he walked away. When he was about ready to leave his view, he called after him. "Hey."

Jaron stopped and turned, raising his eyebrows.

"I thought maybe I'd give Bobby a riding lesson when he gets off the bus. You got any objections?"

"No. I'll bring him out to you after his snack."

Travis nodded.

Jaron turned again.

"Hey." Travis stopped him, a smile playing on his lips.

Jaron turned again, his exasperation clear. "What?"

"Your dog needs a name."

"Bobby hasn't decided yet. And are you gonna let me get back to work?"

Travis grinned. "Yeah, I'll let you."

Jaron shook his head and turned around. When Travis called out to him again, Jaron waved and yelled, "No."

Travis shook his head and followed Jackson around to the front of the barn.

Travis had been friends with Jackson since they were Bobby's age. He knew Jackson had something to say. "Go ahead. Say whatever it is you need to say and get it over with."

They went into the horse barn.

He followed Jackson over to the stall that held his horse.

The horse stuck his head out, wanting attention.

Jackson stroked the horse's long nose three times before he spoke. "Why didn't you tell me?"

Travis knew what Jackson meant. He hadn't told anyone about his sexual preferences except his father, and that was because the secret built up in his body, making his stomach hurt. He had told his old man everything, holding nothing back. His dad had been the easiest person to tell because he trusted the unconditional love.

That same twisting ache in his gut returned. Of all Travis' friends, Jackson was the one he didn't want to lose. And yeah, Jackson had walked out of bars with just as many men as women. Travis was pretty sure he had a friend-with-benefits thing going on with Brian Stockwell but had never asked to confirm it. Logically, he knew rejection wouldn't happen.

Maybe there was something about saying the words out loud to someone who could walk away. Everyone on the farm counted as family. Family accepted and loved without question. His father had plowed that sentiment into every acre of the farm. He'd planted the seed and watched every vine wrap around them all until they understood and opened themselves up.

The lesson had been easy for Travis because he'd grown up with it. That lesson had been why he stayed friends with Brad even though he was an asshole sometimes and that asshole had rubbed off on Jackson when they were younger. But Jackson wasn't that impressionable kid anymore. He'd made up his mind somewhere along the way.

Travis met his gaze, wanting Jackson to see he wouldn't back down from the truth. "Didn't matter until I saw Jaron. Dad died, and you know I had problems after that. Meaningless sex doesn't interest me. Doesn't matter who it's with or their gender."

"What's different about Jaron?"

Travis smiled. "Besides the fact that he's fucking sexy, you mean?"

"He is pretty. But yeah, besides that."

"He's smarter than me. Quicker witted. And doesn't cut me any slack. When he takes a stand, he doesn't back down. He'd die for Bobby." Travis stuck his hands into the pockets of his coat. "There's a thousand other things."

"You're in love with him." It wasn't a question. Jackson knew him well enough not to ask.

Travis answered him anyway. "Yes. Probably from the first moment I saw him in the grocery store. I love Bobby too."

Jackson went in for a hug. "Happy for you, man. And I have your back."

Travis returned the hug. "I appreciate it. Wanna help give Bobby a riding lesson? Maybe Jaron won't freak out as much if there's two of us."

"It's understandable. He didn't grow up on the back of a horse like we did." Jackson pulled back, ending the hug and shrugged. "You got room for a couple more horses?"

Travis winced. "Your dad's getting worse."

It wasn't a question, and Jackson didn't take it as one. He didn't speak right away. "He forgets how to work the computer most times, so I put all our contacts on it. That will stop him from selling any more of our stock for a while." Jackson ran a hand down his face. "It wouldn't be so bad if he remembered what decade he's in and didn't sell horses we don't have anymore. Or sell them so damn cheap. Thankfully, he doesn't make training appointments for me. I hope he doesn't start."

"What do the doctors say?"

Jackson rubbed at the back of his neck. "That Alzheimer's sucks and they're sorry. They push meds and stopped telling us what to expect."

Travis put a hand on his shoulder, squeezing gently to show his support. "We have plenty of room for as long as you need."

"Thanks, man."

They made their way out of the barn as Jaron came around the corner.

Jaron smiled at them both but didn't stop to chat.

Travis kept his gaze on Jaron's ass. The jeans he wore hugged it just right, making the view spectacular.

"Yep. I see the appeal."

Travis elbowed him without looking away. "Are you looking at his ass?"

"Aren't you?"

Jaron bent over to put his half-bushel of cauliflower next to the front door. "Oh, yeah. I should punch you for looking."

"But you can't blame a guy for appreciating."

"Not at all."

Chapter Eighteen

The inside of Travis' truck smelled like him. The subtle spice in his aftershave and a little bit of the garden hung in the air around Jaron as he drove back from his mom's house. A duffle bag full of a weekend's worth of clothing rode shotgun beside him. Maybe it was a little presumptuous to have more than one night's worth. He'd pack it all up and move into Travis' house if he knew for sure it wouldn't set Bobby back. Bobby had come a long way. The fact that he'd stayed with Travis when Jaron left to get their stuff proved that. Of course, Travis had Bobby's full attention with the horse lesson, so that helped.

Travis had Jaron's full attention too.

Jaron smiled and tapped his fingers on the steering wheel. He wanted things he'd never really thought about before. And yeah, maybe the other shoe would drop at some point, and Travis would break his heart, but he planned to live in the moment.

Jaron's smiled died when he turned down the Heath's driveway and saw Bobby on the back of a horse. Travis stood inside the circular corral against the fence on one side, and Jackson stood on the other. The horse walked around in the middle with Bobby on its back. Bobby had leather reins in his hand and a huge smile on his face.

Jaron parked the truck and shut off the engine. He didn't take the time to get the duffle bag out of the truck. Instead, he made a beeline straight for Bobby.

His distress must have shown on his face, because Travis climbed over the wooden fence and closed the distance between them before Jaron could reach the rink. Jaron tried to get around Travis, but he blocked him. "Don't make him scared of horses just because you are."

"I'm not scared of horses, Travis." Okay, that was a lie. The size of a horse intimidated him enough that he wouldn't ever ride one.

Travis gave him a disbelieving look. When Greg came out of the horse barn, Travis turned. Jaron saw it as an opening and made to go around Travis again, but Travis thwarted his efforts with a hand on his shoulder. "Hey Greg, would you do me a favor and saddle Rupert?"

"Sure, boss." Greg went back into the barn, disappearing in the dark.

When Travis turned, he bent, getting right in Jaron's face. The eye contact was unavoidable when Travis held him by the shoulders. Travis kept the grip firm but gentle. "I know I told you I'd ride with him the first couple times, but he's learning quicker than that. The kid's a natural, probably because he doesn't fear them. The second that changes is when he's gonna get hurt."

Jaron narrowed his eyes. "That horse weighs a ton."

"A little over a thousand pounds, actually." Travis smiled as if he thought Jaron's attitude ridiculous. "Poca is the gentlest horse I have."

Jaron crossed his arms over his chest and didn't say a word. His eyes widened when Greg led a big chestnut horse over to them and handed the reins to Travis.

Travis had to pry Jaron's arms apart, but when he did, he held his hand and put it to the horse's nose. "This is Rupert. He's big but gentle. Nothing but sunshine and rainbows for Rupert here."

"Hey Jackson, you got things covered over there?"

Jackson raised a hand. "Bobby, Poca, and I are just fine. You two go have fun."

"Bring Bobby to my house after you're done, will ya?"

"Yep." Jackson never took his eyes off Bobby. "Can you turn her on your own like Travis showed you?"

Bobby nodded, and then concentrated. A second later the horse turned around as if on its own. Bobby smiled down at Jackson.

"Yep, you'll be training horses before ya know it." Jackson took his hat off and closed the distance to Bobby. The horse stopped, and Jackson put his hat on Bobby's head. The thing fell around his eyes, but Jackson adjusted it. "Now you're a proper cowboy."

Bobby beamed. When he reached up to touch the hat with one hand, Jaron sucked in a breath. He wanted to shut his eyes against the horror of Bobby falling off. When he stayed on, Jaron breathed again.

Travis chuckled. "See. Told ya. Natural." Jaron turned his gaze on him, narrowing his eyes again but didn't speak. If he opened his mouth, he'd yell, and the horse Bobby sat on might spook. "It's your turn for a lesson. Come on."

Jaron would have taken a step back if not for Travis gripping his arm. "No way."

Travis pulled him closer until he was close enough to put an arm around his waist. "We'll ride together. You'll be perfectly safe. I promise."

"Is Bobby safe with Jackson?" Jaron hated to ask, but he didn't know Jackson. Not really, anyway. Jaron would trust him if Travis did, but he still didn't like leaving Bobby with a stranger.

"Perfectly. If you want anyone teaching Bobby how to ride, it's Jackson. But I'll keep our ride short if you want."

Oh God. "Okay." Jaron shut his eyes and shored up his courage. When he opened his eyes, Travis kissed him.

Travis let him go, chuckling. He guided Jaron around until they stood next to the horse. "Put your left foot in the stirrup."

Travis let go of the horse's reins and gripped Jaron around the waist.

Jaron did as he directed, grabbing for the saddle horn when Travis lifted him. Jaron sucked in a breath and slung his leg over. The horse shifted underneath him, and he held his breath, letting out a little whimper.

Travis handed him the reins. "Scoot forward, baby."

Jaron couldn't move. Every brain cell in his head shut down and all he could think about was the fact that he had control of a gigantic animal. And it didn't scare Bobby at all? How?

Travis moved his foot out of the stirrup and gripped the saddle horn before swinging up into the saddle.

The horse moved again, shuffling on his feet to get used to the weight.

Travis wrapped a hand around Jaron's waist.

Jaron waited for him to take the reins, but he didn't. He felt Travis' breath on the back of his neck.

"Rupert knows English better than some humans. He also knows how to read your body, so you'll need to relax in your seat. The tighter your legs, the more he thinks he'll need to walk."

"That's why he keeps moving around?" Jaron confused the poor guy. He leaned against Travis, his back to Travis' front, and let his legs relax. Sure enough, Rupert stopped shuffling around. "If he knows how to do all that, why do we need the reins?"

Travis chuckled. "With Rupert, we don't really. Most of the time they're just used to give us more control."

"So Rupert is a smart horse."

"He had a good trainer." Travis pointed to Jackson. "Rupert is Jackson's horse. His baby."

"Why does he keep him here?"

"His dad has Alzheimer's disease. Diagnosed a couple of years after Jackson graduated high school. He's getting worse but still wants to help around the farm. He sells horses they don't even own anymore. Jackson's afraid he'll accidentally sell Rupert. He keeps others here too."

"That's horrible about his dad." Jaron looked Jackson's way, seeing him in a new light.

"Yeah, it's tough on Jackson." Travis made a clicking noise in his throat, and Rupert started walking.

Jaron tried not to stiffen. His heart pounded, hard and fast. The longer the horse walked at a leisurely pace, the more relaxed Jaron got. "So you just click, and he walks."

"Yep. If you smooch, he trots. We won't ask him to do that, though. Telling him to whoa will get him to stop." Rupert slowed down as soon as Travis said it. Travis chuckled and clicked again. "To turn him I use my feet and legs."

"Okay."

"You let me do the turning for now, though."

"Okay."

Travis must have used his feet because Rupert turned, heading to the fields.

"This is peaceful."

"And now that you're on a horse, you're more comfortable with Bobby being on one."

"Yes. Smart ass."

Travis chuckled. "Being right wasn't the goal."

"I know. You're looking out for Bobby." Jaron would have stood in Bobby's way at some point. They both knew it. "Thank you."

Travis kissed Jaron on the cheek. "You don't have to thank me for looking out for Bobby. I always will. The kid won't be able to get rid of me now."

Jaron turned his face up, rubbing his cheek against Travis'. "You're great."

Travis chuckled. "You say that like you're surprised."

"I didn't know you in high school. We never had much to do with each other."

"I didn't pay attention to much more than alcohol in high school."

"Your friends were assholes." Jaron smiled. The skin on his neck held a warmth he wanted to curl up against and cuddle.

"Sometimes they still are. Jackson not so much anymore."

"Why is that?"

"He grew up a lot since his dad became ill. He and I have that in common."

Jaron tilted his face up, wanting a kiss, which Travis gave him, although the angle was awkward. "He's family." Jaron began to understand that Travis thought of anyone close to him as family.

They walked Rupert up into the yard of a big lodge cabin-type home with huge windows making up half of the front, and a porch that wrapped around two sides. A grill and picnic table sat on the porch along with a blue rocking chair. Through the windows, Jaron made out a gray fireplace, but not much else because the windows were tinted just enough that the low lighting didn't allow for it. With the forest as a backdrop, the house was the perfect picture of a cozy home.

"This is your house?"

"Your house now and our house soon."

Travis stopped Rupert in the center of the yard and got down.

Jaron followed his lead, Travis helping him with hands around his waist.

"How was the riding lesson?" Travis pressed against him, Jaron's back to Travis' front. His arms snaked around Jaron's waist, and he held him close.

Jaron leaned into the embrace. His hands slipped away from Rupert's saddle. He placed them over Travis' where they met at his middle. He forgot about everything except the way Travis made him feel. "I feel like we've been dancing around each other forever."

Travis kissed his cheek. "Since that day in the grocery store."

"Yeah. Probably." Jaron turned in Travis' arms, facing him. "What do you say we do something about it tonight?"

Travis' eyes sparkled with mischief, and his arms tightened. "I'd say the anticipation is gonna kill me."

Jaron grinned. "Would a kiss keep you alive?"

"It would help."

Jaron placed a hand on the back of Travis' neck, pulling him down. When their lips met, Jaron didn't waste time with slow. He licked across Travis' lips, letting him know what he wanted. When Travis licked back, Jaron opened, inviting him to take the kiss to the next level.

Travis didn't tease but let Jaron know exactly what he'd like to happen next. Naked and horizontal came to mind, ramping up the desire. He trailed a hand down Jaron's back, running it over his ass.

Jaron whimpered and rose onto his toes, wanting more, wanting Travis' touch on his bare skin. It didn't help, so he tightened his grip on Travis' neck, trying to get him closer but they were already mashed against each other. Still, Jaron wanted to crawl inside Travis and live there forever. Nothing short of that would satisfy him.

"Go home, Rupert." Jackson's voice made Jaron jump.

He ended the kiss and turned to see Jackson holding Bobby's hand as they walked into the yard.

Rupert moved away from them, going right over to Jackson. He stood in front of Jackson and Bobby, nudging Jackson on the chest with his nose.

Bobby giggled. "Why is he doing that?"

Jackson had nothing but affection for the horse. That much was clear. "He wants my attention. Wants to go for a ride." Jackson petted Rupert on the nose. "And don't think I didn't notice you're still here instead of back in the barn."

Bobby's face lit up. "We can go for a ride?" Jaron knew at that moment that he'd never get the kid off a horse again.

Jackson met Jaron's gaze as if asking permission to take Bobby for a trail ride. Jaron nodded.

The puppy growling got his attention. He looked down to see him pulling at Travis' pant leg. "I don't think he likes you so close to me."

"He best get used to it." Travis grinned and reached down, lifting the dog into his arms. He handed the pup to Jaron and walked over to Bobby.

Jackson swung up into the saddle and then reached for Bobby when Travis lifted him. Rupert walked back the way they had come. "You two got an hour before we're back."

Chapter Nineteen

The house had an open floor plan with stairs directly across from the front door. The furnishing matched everything else and had a masculine feel to it. All dark wood and dark colors with a couch and chair designed for comfort. The kitchen stood off to the left with an island separating it from everything else. Three leather-covered stools were tucked against the back side of the island. A table sat over to the side, near a display of windows that looked out into the backyard and forest beyond. Jaron envisioned a small vegetable garden and maybe some roses along the forest line right outside the windows.

"This is a beautiful home." Jaron felt at home in Travis' space, which should have scared him. He had passed the point where Travis breaking his heart would affect his decisions, going forward.

"It got a whole lot better with you in it." Travis held his hand, pulling him toward the stairs. "I'll give you the grand tour after I show you the bedroom."

Jaron would have chuckled at Travis' comment, but he felt the urgency too. His blood heated with each step they took. "Yeah, that's a good plan."

Travis hadn't made the bed. Jaron pictured Travis in it, all naked and warm. He had memories of a naked Travis to fall back on already,

Chapter Twenty

♥

A series about catching snakes in South Africa held everyone's attention.

Travis would classify the man catching the snakes as a brave idiot, but he probably saved people's lives. Especially the little children who ran around in brightly colored shirts and bare feet. He rubbed his thumb across Jaron's arm even as his gaze trailed to the recliner. Jackson had the plush chair stretched out and his big sleeping form was equally as stretched out. Bobby lay on him, having fallen asleep first. "Those two made fast friends."

"Jackson's an easy person to like. He was in high school, too." Jaron smirked. "Not for me, but most everyone else."

Travis kissed Jaron on the temple and thought about the last part of what Jaron said. "Jackson worshipped Brad back then."

"Everyone did. He supplied the alcohol." Jaron met his gaze, shaking his head. "Anyone who drinks as much as Brad did in high school used it to drown out something."

Travis lifted his eyebrows at Jaron's perceptiveness.

"Tracy self-medicated. A lot. She had a traumatic childhood and never really dealt with it properly." Jaron leaned into Travis. "As shitty as her life had been growing up, she still managed to protect Bobby at the end. I'll always be grateful to her for that."

"You miss her." Travis hadn't asked about Tracy, and he should have. Jaron needed to talk about her and what happened if he wanted to come to terms with it. Travis remembered that stage of grief. The struggle for acceptance had been the hardest for Travis to get through and maybe in a lot of ways he still hadn't accepted his father's death.

"I think about her every day."

"Yeah. That won't change." Travis smiled. "Dad would have liked seeing Bobby today. I can practically hear him in my mind. 'That kid has something special. He'll be training show horses before you know it. You mark my words.'"

Jaron smiled. "Tracy would have liked seeing him on the horses too. She always thought I coddled him too much. Maybe she was right."

"Nah, Bobby needs a balance. She helped create that."

Jaron turned his face up and kissed Travis. "So did you today."

Travis met Jaron's gaze, studying him. "And how do you feel about that?"

"You said you wouldn't push Bobby away if things didn't work out between you and me. I trust you."

Jaron might have used the word *if* but he meant *when*. As much as that rankled, Travis couldn't do anything about it but stay the course. The last thing he wanted to do was comment on Jaron's lack of faith and start an argument. Instead, he changed the subject. "You getting hungry?"

Jaron nodded and smiled. "When Bobby and Jackson wake up, they probably will be too. No doubt all that riding worked off a lot of calories."

Travis' cooking skills needed work, but he could grill a steak okay. He bet Jaron did a better job, though. Cupping Jaron's cheek, he stared into his eyes. "I'll make it worth your while if you make dinner."

Jaron snorted out a laugh. "How?"

Travis wiggled his eyebrows. "With more alone time."

"We'll do that even if I don't make dinner. Try again."

"Maybe that's all I have."

Jaron pursed his lips and stood. "Not good enough."

"Not good enough. Why you..." Travis went for a playful swat at Jaron's butt, growling.

Jaron dodged at the last minute, running for the door as he did. Travis gave chase, which was probably what Jaron's aim had been all along. He laughed as he left out of the front door, running across the yard. Travis closed the distance between them easily.

When Travis wrapped his arms around Jaron, he laughed like a loon. Travis worked it so Jaron lay underneath him on the ground. He held Jaron's arms over his head.

"You're getting me dirty." Jaron chuckled through the words.

"Getting you dirty is the fun part."

"Travis." Jaron squirmed around, trying to upend him.

Travis held firm, grinning the whole time. He held Jaron's wrists in one hand, freeing up his other to tickle.

Jaron laughed, wiggling around even more, trying to get away from the gentle torture, all the while screaming in laughter. His shirt bunched around Travis' hand as he tickled Jaron's side.

At some point, the puppy grabbed hold of Travis' sleeve and pulled at it.

And then he had a boy lying across his back. He stopped tickling Jaron long enough to see Bobby smiling at him, his blue eyes sparkling with mischief.

"I know what I want to name the puppy."

"What is it?" Jaron's face flushed, and he still chuckled.

"Brownie. Jackson said it fits." Bobby turned his head toward Jackson over his shoulder. "It fits, right?"

"Yep." Jackson chuckled from where he stood, leaning against the porch railing.

When Bobby turned back to them, he looked at Jaron, his expression turning serious. "Papa, I'm hungry."

"Travis and I were negotiating dinner. I'll be right in as soon as I get what I want."

Bobby climbed off him. "Huh-oh. That means Papa's gonna yell. Probly."

Travis tickled him again. "You gonna yell, baby?"

Jaron laughed hysterically and shook his head.

"Are you gonna make dinner?" Travis stopped until Jaron caught his breath.

Jaron grinned and shook his head again, so Travis continued his torture. "Okay. Okay."

"And what's your price?" The next time Travis stopped tickling Jaron, he worked his hand up to cup Jaron's cheek. "My attention later?"

"A bath in that whirlpool tub you have. And your attention."

"Deal." Travis let Jaron go. When he stood, he pulled Jaron up with him and led him back into the house.

Jaron went right to the kitchen and pulled the refrigerator door open.

Travis sat on one of the stools.

Bobby wanted on the stool next to him, so Travis helped, picking him up and settling him in the seat.

Jackson sat on the stool next to Bobby.

Jaron had spices and red meat in front of him, but he didn't prep them. Instead, he met each one of their gazes. "You guys need a job to do."

"I'm fine right here. I like watching you." Travis winked.

"Me too. The view is rather cute." Jackson grinned.

Reaching around Bobby, Travis smacked Jackson in the back of the head. He didn't hit him hard enough to hurt, and that was confirmed when Jackson chuckled. "Stop flirting with my man."

Jaron blushed. He tried to brush off the effects of Travis and Jackson's teasing with an eye roll, but he didn't quite succeed. "Jackson, will you go start the grill?"

"Sure thing, cutie." Jackson's stool slid across the floor.

Travis stood when he passed and grabbed Jackson around the neck in a headlock. The dog barked at their roughhousing and Bobby giggled in delight. "Get your own guy. Leave mine alone."

"I would, but yours is so pretty."

Travis tightened his hold, making Jackson chuckle.

"Travis, let Jackson go and make a salad." Jaron's dad voice laced through the command.

Letting Jackson go, he pushed him on the shoulder when he straightened up.

Jackson chuckled and headed outside.

Travis plucked Bobby off the stool. "What goes in a salad, little man?"

Bobby looked to Jaron for the answer.

Jaron smiled at him. "All the veggies."

Bobby met his gaze again and looked at Travis expectantly. "I think we can manage that. But first, we gotta give your dad a kiss."

"Because you like him?"

Travis knelt, getting on Bobby's level. "I have a secret." He crooked a finger as he whispered the comment. Travis winked at Jaron when their gazes met.

Bobby's arm came around Travis' shoulder, and he leaned against him. "I can know?"

Travis nodded. "I more than like your dad."

"Do you more than like me too?"

"Oh yeah. We're full on to love, you and I." Travis kissed Bobby's cheek.

Bobby grinned and nodded before hugging him.

Travis lifted him into his arms.

Bobby laid his head on Travis' shoulder and stuck his thumb into his mouth.

Travis closed the distance between them and Jaron.

Jaron had all kinds of emotions floating around in his gaze. Before he could voice any of them, Travis gripped his nape with his free hand and pulled Jaron in for a kiss. It was just a press of the lips and not designed to heat the blood. When he pulled back, he said, "I meant every word. Just so we're clear."

"Okay."

Bobby pulled his thumb out of his mouth and grabbed Jaron's face in both of his hands. He planted one on him quickly before letting him go. "Now we make a salad?"

Chapter
Twenty-One

♥

After spending all weekend waking up without an alarm, with Travis snuggled close to him, the incessant beeping seemed foreign to his brain. Jaron groaned and pulled Travis' hand up his chest to his ear, using it to block out the sound.

Travis took his hand away, and his body moved over Jaron just long enough to shut off the alarm. They both settled when the quiet surrounded them again.

He'd always fallen asleep fast, never one to linger awake for even a few minutes once his head hit the pillow. More often than not, he ended up roaming the house at all hours of the early morning. With Travis in bed with him, he'd learned to like lingering.

Lips brushed against his hair. Jaron smiled without opening his eyes.

"What do you say we play hooky and lie in bed all day? We can make Jackson bring us food," Travis said into his hair.

"Sounds great. But Bobby has to go to school. And your mom might fire me."

"You don't realize Jackson's full potential as our servant. Plus, my mom thinks you walk on water, so you're golden there."

"What about the ranch?"

"Jackson can do that, too."

Jackson had yet to leave except to get some clothes. For some reason, he didn't want to go back home, and Jaron thought it might have something to do with his ill father. He didn't blame Jackson for needing a break. It turned out Jackson was a fun, likable guy, so Jaron wasn't complaining.

The door to their room banged open, and Bobby barreled inside, jumping on the bed beside Jaron. "Jackson said for me to tell you to get up."

"Tell Jackson to go fall off a cliff," Travis said, burrowing into Jaron's warmth.

"'K" Bobby ran from the room. "Jackson! They said for you to go fall off a cliff."

"Be careful on the stairs, Bobby." Jaron pictured him tumbling halfway down because he decided to run everywhere he went. "Slow down!"

"I am!" Bobby's voice carried through the entire house.

Jaron was instantly cold when Travis got out of bed. He watched as Travis slipped off his pajama pants and underwear, putting them into the hamper before walking across the room to the bathroom. God, he was beautiful.

Travis had a slight smile on his face as if he knew what Jaron thought. That mischievous sparkle entered his eyes as he went into the bathroom, leaving the door open, so Jaron had a clear view inside. He opened the shower door and faced away from Jaron as he adjusted the water, giving Jaron a clear view of his ass.

Jaron got out of bed and closed the distance between them. He ran his hands over the smooth globes. "This is about the only thing that would get me out of bed."

Travis chuckled. "You need encouragement."

Jaron smiled and gave Travis one more pat before going over to the toilet.

Travis went into the shower and shut the door, while Jaron relieved his bladder.

"Would you be able to take me to my mom's house? I want to pack some of my stuff." Jaron had every intention of following through on his slow-moving strategy, but Bobby didn't seem bothered by the weekend sleepover. The exact opposite was the case. He loved the farm and came out of his shell around Travis and Jackson. Both men were talkative and outgoing, and Bobby seemed to crave the attention. As for Jaron, he wanted to wake up next to Travis more often.

"Of course, baby. I can drop Bobby off at school too."

"Thank you." Jaron washed his hands and dried them before pulling the shower door open. Water cascaded down Travis' body and his hair slicked back, all wet and shiny, the color turning a deep red. Jaron leaned in far enough for a wet kiss but not far enough to get himself wet. He received what he desired. "I'm going to make Bobby breakfast. See you in ten."

"Sure thing, sweetness."

"Okay, sugar plum."

Travis' laughter followed Jaron down the stairs.

Bobby already sat on one of the stools with a bowl of cereal in front of him and a spoon in his hand.

Jackson chose to feed Bobby the small circled cereal with no added sugar. He also made coffee.

Jackson sat beside Bobby, eating the same thing. He was fully dressed and had showered at some point.

Jaron poured a cup for himself and took a sip, closing his eyes at the goodness. It woke his body a little. "Bless you."

Jackson snorted out a chuckle. "I'm that good, huh?"

"Better." Jaron nodded to Bobby's bowl. "You made the right cereal choice too."

"Well, I'm gonna eat, brush my teeth, and then I'm out of your hair for a few days."

Jaron frowned. "But Bobby and I don't want you to leave."

Jackson rustled Bobby's hair and smiled. "I have to check on things at my farm. Make sure Dad and the stepmom are getting on fine. But I'll come back and stay as long as you're cool with it."

"More than cool. I'll clean out the dresser and closet in your room to prove it." Travis called the room Jackson used *the spare room*, but Jaron thought of it as Jackson's.

Jackson smiled. "You don't have to do that."

"I know. But I'm gonna anyway." If Jaron could make Jackson's life a bit easier by making space for him, then it was a small thing.

Whatever reprieve staying with them had given Jackson was over. The resignation came through in Jackson's gaze. "Thanks."

"We're staying here too, right Papa?"

Jaron smiled. "Do you want to?"

Bobby nodded. "With Travis?"

"He'll sleep over sometimes."

Bobby frowned. "But not all the time?"

"No. Not all the time."

"Why?"

"Because Travis and Papa need…" Jaron narrowed his eyes at Jackson when he laughed again. "Just because. Okay, Bobby."

"But, Why?"

"It's a complicated answer."

Jackson grinned before answering for him. "Because your Papa wants to pretend Travis won't be here every night. It gives him the illusion of taking things slow even though neither one of them will or even wants to. Ain't that right, Jaron?"

Jaron shook his head. "Shut up."

Jackson chuckled and stood with his empty bowl. He walked around the island to the sink and rinsed it out before patting Jaron's shoulder. "It's all right with me if you want to keep fooling yourself."

"Thanks. Because I needed your approval."

Jackson snorted out a chuckle again and headed into the bathroom.

Jaron had the window cracked open about an inch. The cool morning air filtered inside the truck cab. Fall had set in enough that some of the leaves on the trees turned a pretty yellow, mixing with the green. He turned to the cows milling about in the field to the left. They were all black and smaller than the black and white ones, which held the majority on the Heath farm. "What kind of cows are those?"

"Angus. Beef cattle. That fellow right there." Travis pointed to one that stood a few feet from the rest. "That's the bull. The rest are cows."

"So he's got a job to do. Looks like he's not doing much but standing around."

"He's pacing himself. Can only impregnate one at a time." Travis took Jaron's hand in his and laced their fingers together.

"Papa," Bobby said from the backseat.

"Yes." Jaron gave Travis a knowing look. "Here it comes."

"I love you. And I think I should stay home today. Brownie might get lonely."

"I love you too. Brownie is coming to work with me like he always does."

"I think I should go with Travis. You need my help?"

"No." Jaron didn't wait for Travis to answer.

Travis chuckled but otherwise didn't comment.

It took Bobby a full two minutes before he changed gears. "I love you, Travis."

Travis' eyebrows went up. "I love you too. But I can't help you, little man. Sorry."

"You can take me for ice cream after school at least?"

Travis met Jaron's gaze. "I could pick him up from school and take him to the place in town. That okay with you?"

"Yeah." Jaron bit his bottom lip and decided it was as good a time as any to bring up the next topic. "I'd like to add you to Bobby's emergency contacts and pick up lists. I mean, if it's okay with you. You don't have to or anything. I just thought that maybe just in case something was to come up. An emergency or something. And I don't have a car so..."

Travis squeezed his hand. "I want to be on the list, Jaron. Of course."

Jaron sighed in relief. "It's just that things are moving fast, and I don't want to pressure you."

"Doesn't matter what happens between you and me. I told you that before." Travis pulled up into the school parking lot. "You need to slow down?"

"No. That's not what I'm saying." Jaron had passed the time where he'd save his heart. If Travis broke it than he did. And he trusted Travis when he said he wouldn't break Bobby's heart. That's all that mattered.

"Okay. Best get in there and add me then."

Jaron smiled and opened the truck door.

Bobby climbed out of the booster seat on his own.

Jaron opened his door and grabbed the backpack that Bobby had forgotten as he got out.

Jaron took Bobby's hand as they made their way through the cars dropping off kids.

"I have a secret."

Jaron handed Bobby the backpack when they got to the front door. He squatted down. "What is it?"

"I don't like school."

"That's not a secret because everyone knows."

Bobby sighed. "You're gonna make me go."

Jaron nodded. "Yep."

A small dark-haired boy stopped beside them. He smiled at Bobby. "Will you play with me at recess?"

"Okay." And just like that Bobby lit up. He followed the boy into the school, leaving Jaron outside.

It took less than a minute to add Travis to the list. The secretary pulled a file and wrote down his name and phone number. "Also, I'd like him to ride the bus to school as well."

"At the Heath farm?"

"Yes, ma'am."

She wrote down Bobby's name on a list with the Heath's address and then smiled at him. "You're all set."

"Thank you, ma'am."

"Have a nice day, Jaron."

"You too, Mrs. Bell." Jaron walked out, dodging kids and parents as he went. He made his way across the parking lot to Travis' truck.

Jaron must have had an expression on his face because the second he climbed in Travis chuckled. "He made a last-ditch effort, didn't he?"

Jaron shook his head and laughed. "I hope that kid learns to like school as much as he likes the farm."

"I doubt that will ever happen, baby."

"Me too. But at least he's here. And he found a friend."

Getting out of the school parking lot, wasn't as easy as getting in. They had to wait in line for everyone else dropping kids off. "Bobby will ride the bus to school starting tomorrow. Not just home anymore."

Travis' gaze snapped to him, and his mouth opened.

"What?"

"You called the farm 'home'."

"Was I not supposed to?" Jaron stiffened and averted his gaze, facing forward. "Cars are pulling up."

Travis gripped the back of his neck and pulled him in for a kiss. Travis kept the kiss light, pecking him on the lips. "You were supposed to say what you did."

Jaron smiled. "Okay."

Someone honked behind them. Travis pulled the car forward. He rolled down the window and waved at whoever was behind them.

Someone yelled, "Stop sucking his face and pay attention, Heath."

Everyone in the car line probably heard. Jaron wanted to crawl in a hole somewhere. It was one thing to know everyone in town knew they were dating and another to have that knowledge yelled across the elementary school parking lot.

Travis didn't seem worried if his grin was any indication. He stuck his head out and looked behind him. "Why would I pay attention to you when I have him beside me, Gagliardo?"

Ian Gagliardo had graduated a year behind them and had played football well enough that everyone thought he'd go to college on a scholarship. He'd gotten Michelle Withrow pregnant their junior year, and that changed his life. Everyone said it was a shame that happened. That Ian was destined for greatness. Even Jaron thought that back when the knowledge had been fresh. His perspective changed the day Bobby had been born.

Jaron turned to see Ian behind them. He waved, smiling at Ian, before turning around again. Ian didn't seem as if he minded the way his life had turned out.

"Call me later. We'll set up a play date for the kids," Ian yelled.

Travis waved at that and turned back around. "Will do, man."

Travis met Jaron's gaze but broke it when the cars pulled forward again. It was their turn at the road, which held most of Travis' attention. "You okay?"

It was an odd thing to ask. "I'm fine. Why?"

"You just had a look is all."

Jaron shrugged. "I didn't expect the acceptance."

"Ian's a good dude."

"What about everyone else in line?"

Travis pulled out onto the road before giving Jaron a look. "What about them?"

"They all know we're dating. They probably heard about you and Brad fighting."

"Are you telling me you want to hide?"

Jaron narrowed his eyes. "Hell no. I'm not the one who came out recently. I'm just making sure you understand."

Travis grabbed his hand and held it up to his lips, kissing the center of his palm. "I'm not going anywhere, baby."

"People can be shitheads, Travis."

Travis laced their fingers together and rested them on the center console. "I'm not going anywhere, and I'll keep saying that until you believe it."

Jaron didn't believe it.

Instead of creating an argument, Jaron changed the subject. "I have to pack some more stuff. I'll be quick."

His mother's car sat in the driveway. She should have been at work. The fact that she wasn't meant a quick run inside wasn't in the cards.

"If you need to go back to the farm, you can." Jaron pointed to his mother's car. "I'll be a while."

She may very well flip her gourd when Jaron told her he was going to move into Travis' house.

"You don't have to move. If you think it's not the right time, then maybe you shouldn't." Travis' jaw ticced, and he looked anywhere but at Jaron.

"Do you want me to?" Jaron knew what Travis said, but maybe he needed an out. Maybe it was all too much, too fast.

"I like the idea of you close. And like I said, I'm not going any-where."

"I like the idea too."

"But you don't believe me when I say I'm all in."

"I'm halfway there."

Travis sighed. "Do you want me to go?"

"If you want to."

"Jaron. Damn it, tell me what you want. If you want me to go, I'll go." Travis hadn't ever raised his voice before. At least not at Jaron.

"I don't want you to go."

"Do you need me to help carry things?"

"Yes. And I want you there for moral support. But can you wait until after I talk to my mom before you come in."

Travis finally smiled. "I can do that."

"And I'm sorry."

"You still won't trust me, though."

"I'm trying."

"I know. And I'm trying not to let that bother me."

Jaron sighed. "How about we shelve the conversation."

Travis nodded. "Go in and argue with your mom. Sounds better than arguing with me."

"Very funny."

"But accurate." Travis shooed him with his hand.

Jaron closed the distance between them. He gripped the back of Travis' neck, pulling up closer. "I know enough about you to know I want to see where this thing goes. I'm not worried about the future. I think maybe I should be. I've spent a lot of time with a woman who said one thing but always did another."

Travis smiled, but it didn't quite reach his eyes. "That is not me."

Jaron kissed Travis but kept it quick. "I do know that, Travis."

"Go have your talk." Travis cupped his cheek, and they kissed again.

They hadn't solved any problems, but they'd solved it enough to create a sweet moment. Jaron didn't want to leave that.

Travis let him go, and Jaron got out of the truck.

Jaron yelled for his mother as soon as he went into the house. "Mom!"

"I'm right here. Why are you yelling?" Jaron followed the sound of her voice.

"Oh. Sorry." He closed the door behind him and made his way through the kitchen to the living room. He sat next to her on the couch, turning so he faced her. "Are you okay?"

"Yeah." Her expression suggested she thought him crazy for asking. "Why wouldn't I be?"

"You're home from work."

"I had to take a vacation day. If I didn't, I'd lose it." She turned as well, sitting the way he was. "How was your weekend?"

"Great. Travis is outside waiting for me. I can't take long, but I need to talk to you about something." Travis had stuff to do on the farm and Jaron had a house to clean. They both needed to get to work sooner rather than later so small talk with his mother wasn't on the agenda.

"If you tell me you're leaving Pickleville again I will be very angry, Jaron McAllister." She gave him the mom stare. She had given him that penetrating stare more often than not growing up. It's how he knew she meant business.

"No, I'm just moving closer to my job."

The relief on her face was visible. "Oh, thank God."

"I'm sorry I scared you, Mom."

She hugged him, her arms tightening around him a bit too much as if she feared he'd disappear if she didn't hold him tight enough. She smiled when she let him go. "Tell me all about it."

"Well, Travis offered to let me rent his house, which is just a small walk from the big house. So I'm moving Bobby and me there."

"What if you break it off with him? Then you're moving Bobby back home again." She made a valid point, and it was one he had thought of already.

"I want to look online for a renter's agreement or something. He said I could pay him if it makes me feel better and it does. I'm going to insist he set a monthly rate that is fair to him. If I don't, he'll set it for ten dollars a month or something."

She let out a sigh as if resigning herself to the inevitable. "Travis is a good boy. He'll give you the shirt of his back if you let him."

Jaron smiled and nodded. "I'm starting to learn that. He's already made Bobby family. So has Bev, for that matter."

She patted his hand. "Best get used to that mentality. The whole Heath lot is like that."

"I just wish I could trust his feelings toward me."

"Give it time and you will." She took a deep breath and squared her shoulders as if she were ready to go to battle. "Now. I have demands."

Jaron's eyebrows went up and he fought not to grin.

"I want to see Bobby at least once a week. Overnight visits. None of this one-day crap. Also, you and I have to go to lunch or something every once in a while. And I want a phone call a couple of times a week."

Jaron laughed. "I'm moving across town, not to the moon, mom."

"I have to make my demands now while you're agreeable."

"Well, would you come to dinner tomorrow night then?"

"I'm looking forward to it." She patted his hand again. "I also want to say how proud I am of you. You've been through a lot lately, and you haven't let that derail you when it comes to Bobby."

"He is my whole world."

She gave him a sad smile. "You're a much better parent to him than I was to you."

Jaron couldn't help the tears that came. She was the only parent he had. He'd always wanted to make her proud, and he'd always felt as if he fell short of the mark. "Thanks, Mom."

"Do you need help packing?"

"I'm only taking a few things today."

"Not fully committing. That's what that means." She gave him that mom stare again, looking into his soul. "It's too late to guard your heart against hurt. You're in love. I can see it every time you talk about him."

Chapter
Twenty-Two

♥

J aron hadn't had a night alone in so long he didn't know what to do with himself. Even though only fifteen minutes had gone by since his mother left with Bobby, that was all it took for boredom to set in, and the silence to take over everything.

He stroked Brownie's back as they sat on the couch. A paperback romance novel about a dragon shifter and an unsuspecting human lay on the coffee table, unopened. He'd turn the television on, but he'd only flip through the channels once or twice and declare it a wasted effort before shutting it off again.

The peace and quiet should have been welcoming. Ever since his mom made the demand to take Bobby overnight, he had been looking forward to it. He had a list of things he wanted to do, starting with reading every book on Travis' shelf, especially the ones he'd recently added. The anticipation far outweighed the reality.

He picked up his phone and texted Travis. *I miss you.*

He hadn't seen Travis, except for glimpses around the farm, in nearly a week.

"You can come in."

Jaron hesitated before sliding the lock mechanism back and opening the stall door. When he stepped inside, he got a visual of Travis' grief. He had red-rimmed eyes and a couple of days' beard growth. Jaron shut the door behind him, reaching through the stall bars to slide the lock into place.

Jaron sat down next to Travis. He took one of Travis' hands in his and laced their fingers together. "Is he...Is there anything I can do to help?"

Travis shook his head. "You're here. That's enough."

"I would have been here sooner had I known."

"Thought you needed space."

"I never said that."

"You didn't have to say those exact words. I got the message." Travis ran his free hand up and down Trick's leg.

Whatever talk they should have Jaron saw Travis didn't need the added stress. Jaron decided to shelf the issue for the time being. "What's wrong with him?"

"He's just old. It's his time."

"He's family."

"Yeah. He's the first horse I ever rode. I think I was four or something when my dad brought him home for me. My dad spent a good few months training him so that he was ready for a beginner rider. Even as young as I was, I remember Dad in the ring outside lunging him. Dad was so patient I think some of that spilled over into Trick because he had been great for kids. I would have taught Bobby on him, but he hasn't felt good for a while. The vet says there's nothing she could do for him anymore."

"I'm sorry." Jaron let go of Travis' hand in favor of putting an arm around him. Travis leaned into him. "Do you need anything? Can I get you something to eat or drink?"

Travis shook his head. "Thanks, baby. I'm good."

Jaron sighed. He wanted to help somehow, and Travis had probably been in the stall for longer than his body needed. Jaron doubted Travis had been taking care of himself properly. "Are you sure?"

"Leonard made me eat." Travis patted a hand on something next to him. "I have a bottle of water here."

Jaron looked around him and saw the light reflect off the metal of a refillable bottle. Leonard's presence on the porch made more sense. He didn't seem the type to hover, but he'd still stay close just in case Travis needed him.

"Tomorrow morning, I have to see a guy about some cattle. I'll be gone overnight at least. Trick will probably be gone by the time I get back, so I wanted to spend tonight with him."

Jaron pulled Travis closer, wanting to relieve some of the anguish. "Can you reschedule the meeting?"

"It'll mean losing money if I do."

"I'll stay with him. Bev will give me the day off for that. I'll stay until he…he won't be alone." Tracy had deserved to have Jaron around the day she died. Maybe she wouldn't have died if he had been there. Maybe two against one would have been the magic number.

Travis pulled Jaron closer.

Jaron settled onto Travis' lap. He removed Travis' hat and laced his fingers through Travis' hair. Their gazes met.

"Thank you."

Jaron nodded.

Travis pressed his lips to Jaron's temple, then moved down to his cheek. "She knows you loved her, baby. You know that, right?"

Jaron sucked in a breath and fought against the lump in his throat. His eyes swam with tears, and then one slid down. He opened his mouth to speak, but nothing came out except a sob. Pressing his cheek to Travis', he let the emotion wash through him. "H-how?"

"Because she's family. Just like Trick is. The love is there regardless of species or whatever the hell."

Jaron sucked down his emotions as best as he could. "I'm sorry."

Travis pulled him back enough, so their gazes met again. "For what?"

"For making this about me. It's not. And I'll stop."

Travis smiled and wiped a tear away from Jaron's cheek with his thumb. "Do you want the bad news or the good news first?"

Okay, Jaron would play along. "Bad, I guess."

"The thing we have the most in common is grief. Sucks."

Jaron smiled. "Yeah, it does."

"The good news is we can help each other through it." Travis wiped his thumb across his other cheek.

"I'm all for that." Jaron cupped Travis' face. "I'm sorry if you felt I pushed you away. I didn't mean to, and I...I'd like it if, when you came back from your business trip, if you'd maybe...spend the night more often. Since it's your bed and all anyway."

Travis kissed him. "We signed a lease agreement. It's your bed now. And I'd like that."

Chapter
Twenty-Three

J aron knee-walked closer to Trick. He petted the horse's belly and watched as the pause in between breaths didn't end. Jaron held his breath, waiting a long second.

He'd never experienced life leaving a body before. He expected the life to go out of the horse like a boom. One single bomb going off, and the end. Instead, it was a slow trickle, like drips from a water faucet until the tub filled.

Travis had left a few hours ago.

Jaron sat against the stall wall and realized he'd have to deliver the bad news. He hadn't thought that far ahead when he'd volunteered to stay. Not that it would have changed anything if he had, but he should have prepared himself. He should have prepared words. Taking a deep breath, he stood. He reached around the stall door for the latch just as he saw Greg coming into the barn. He opened the stall door. "He...he died. Just now."

Greg nodded. "We'll take care of it."

Jaron stepped out of the stall. "Thanks." His hands shook as he fought the urge to go back to Trick. The thought of leaving him turned his stomach. He hesitated and took a step back inside.

Greg put a hand on his shoulder. "I remember you."

Jaron turned back to him, confusion on his face. "What?"

"The day I got my guitar from my parents' house. You asked me if I needed help." *Oh.* Jaron had almost forgotten about that and hadn't put the dots together that the scared boy with the guitar had been Greg.

"Yeah." Jaron tried to smile but couldn't muster one. "I'm glad you're here, where it's safe."

"Leonard told me about you."

Well, that came as a bit of a surprise. Greg didn't say it as if Leonard had said anything bad, so Jaron waited.

"He said you came out in middle school."

Jaron nodded. "Not on purpose, but yeah."

"I graduated last school year. Being out in middle and high school sucks but I didn't get bullied. Neither did any of the others. We had a gay-straight alliance, and the teachers do stuff. Like suspend a bully now."

Jaron smiled. "I'm glad you have a different experience than I did."

"Well, I just want to say thank you."

"For what?"

"For coming out when you did. Probably the reason things changed in the schools." Greg shrugged. "The timing works out. Two and two make four, right?"

"Right." Even as Jaron agreed, he had his doubts. Why would things change because of him? No one had paid that much attention back then. Did they?

Maybe he'd had more eyes on him than he had originally thought.

"I got this in here." Greg patted him on the back again.

Jaron nodded, but he went into Trick's stall. He knelt next to Trick's head and petted his long nose. When he stood and exited the stall, Greg still stood in the same spot, watching him. Jaron smiled at him and walked out of the barn.

Jaron made his way up to the main house, entering from the back door, taking his shoes off as he went. He still had on pajama pants and a red T-shirt from last night. Jaron searched for Beverly throughout the house and found her in the living room, reading on her e-book device.

She smiled at him when he walked in, but it quickly turned to a frown the farther into the room he came. "He's gone."

Jaron nodded.

"My Willis would be so sad. He and Travis loved that horse. I think Trick gave them a deeper bond than most fathers and sons have." She set her reader on the couch beside her and stood.

"Travis said Trick was family."

Beverly smiled. "Yes, well, Travis is his father's son. Through and through." She hugged him but quickly let him go. "How are you doing?"

"I'm okay. Tired. I feel terrible for Travis."

Beverly pointed a finger in the air. "If you feel up to the drive, you should go to him. He'll want you too. You can take one of the farm vehicles if you'd like. I'll print out directions to his hotel before you head out."

Jaron opened his mouth to protest but didn't get any words out before she headed out of the room toward the kitchen. He didn't have any choice but to follow her. It was as she handed him car keys that he finally spoke. "He wouldn't mind?"

"No. He'd love you for the gesture." Beverly smiled and pointed to the table. "Sit. Let me make you some breakfast. Gloria and I will work out who watches Bobby."

Jaron sat at the table and let her take care of him. "Thank you."

"You're a good boy, Jaron McAllister. Travis' father would say anyone who sits with another man's dying horse has a strong character." She smiled.

Beverly started the coffee.

Jaron wanted to rest before he started the drive. It would take at least three hours to get there, and he probably needed a little bit of sleep before he left. He wouldn't, though. Sleep wouldn't come. Maybe she knew that as well so figured the caffeine of the coffee would benefit him instead of hinder. "I wish I could have met him."

"Travis is a lot like him." Beverly pulled eggs out of the refrigerator. "Willis loved this farm. He worried that Travis wouldn't quit being wild long enough to take care of it when needed. Maybe he wouldn't have if Willis hadn't gotten sick. Who knows how it would have gone?"

"Travis stepped up."

"Every day he makes his father proud." She smiled and prepared to scramble more eggs than Jaron could eat in one sitting.

When the coffee finished brewing, she poured him a cup and put it in front of him on the table with a bowl of cream and sugar.

He smiled his thanks and wrapped his fingers around the warm mug.

"Gloria tells me you lost someone. It's why you came back home."

"Yes. Partly why. I'd been thinking about moving back for a while. I didn't want Bobby to go to school in the city. The one near where we lived wouldn't have given him the best education. And I think I was ready for a slower lifestyle. Tracy dying just made the move happen quicker."

"Was Tracy a good mother?"

Jaron smiled. "She did okay when she wasn't getting high. Those moments were few. She loved Bobby, though. No doubt about that."

"Missing them grows with time, not lessens."

Jaron nodded and swallowed down the lump in his throat. "Today just reminds me of the loss." He didn't want to feel the pain anymore but didn't know how to shut it off.

Beverly held the fork up, pointing it at him. "As it should."

Jaron's head snapped up. He felt as if she smacked him.

"Bobby needs to know her. You're the only one who can tell him. You can't bury her memory just because it's painful. For Bobby's sake."

Jaron closed his eyes and sighed. "I know."

Chapter
Twenty-Four

♥

J aron hadn't missed the city at all. The hustle and bustle annoyed him, and his fatigue only made that feeling worse. Everyone had a mission to get from point A to point B as quickly as they could, and god forbid a person stood in the way. When Jaron lived in the city, he didn't drive. He took public transportation. What a wonderful thing that had been to his nerves. Driving sucked. At least he had something to look at besides cornfields and flat land.

He had the directions to the hotel on the seat beside him, but he didn't need them because he saw a sign for the hotel up ahead. The tall building might have blended in well with the rest of its surroundings, but the hotel owners had done a fine job of funneling people right to it.

He pulled into the hotel's parking garage and parked before pulling his cell phone out of his pocket and flipping it open. He sent a text to Travis. *Hey, call me plz.*

He tapped on the wheel for a total of five minutes before he decided to get out of the car. He shut off the engine and pocketed the car keys before grabbing his overnight bag and heading inside the hotel.

In the elevator going down to the hotel lobby, he looked at his phone again. Nothing.

Gotta talk 2 u. Call me.

Each second that went by without a response twisted Jaron's gut. And yeah, he knew he wasn't giving Travis enough time to respond. His impatience wore him to the bone, thinning out his nerves, making him a jittery mess.

The elevator opened into the hotel lobby. The lobby had a sitting area with a couch and a couple of matching plush chairs. A man sat on the couch with his bags at his feet and a newspaper in his hand.

The lobby desk lay straight ahead against the far wall. A restaurant with the hostess standing at a podium lay on the left halfway between the front door and front desk. A noisy bar stood on the other side directly across the large room.

A drink would calm his nerves. He pulled out his phone before entering the bar. No way would he hear it in there, even if the song playing had a slow beat. He headed to it and stood just inside the large open door, letting his eyes adjust to the lighting.

The bar had blue lights and shiny silver everywhere. The after-work crowd had arrived if the number of people drinking and dancing were any indication. Some were at the bar, drinking off the stress of their day. Those were his people, so he closed the distance between himself and the bar. He found an empty stool and sat next to a woman in a dark suit with a glass of wine in her hand. She looked as if she hadn't been able to close an important deal. Her hair hung down past her shoulders, and she sighed several times. She gave him the once over and must have found him uninteresting because she didn't glance his way again.

The bartender had on a black T-shirt that covered lots of muscles. He smiled before speaking. "What can I get you?"

"Beer. Whatever's on tap." Jaron pulled his wallet out of his back pocket and pulled out a bill to cover it and a tip. He held the bill against the bar and scanned the room to give himself something to do while he waited for the drink.

When his gaze made it to the dance floor, he saw Travis. The bag of chips and soda he had bought from the gas station and ate on the way threatened to come up. He took a deep breath and then another. He rubbed at the ache in his chest and pushed down the hurt.

God, Jaron wanted to punch the bitch who held Travis in her arms. But he wouldn't. Because he was a better person than that. Damn it.

He fucking knew it would happen. Travis would break his heart all over the fucking place.

He took a deep breath and turned around, not wanting to look at Travis with his cheek pressed to some bimbo's face and his arms around her waist, holding her as if she meant something to him.

The woman beside him looked from him to Travis and his *date*, then back again before her gaze turned sympathetic.

Jaron ignored her. That proved easy when the bartender placed his drink in front of him. Jaron slid the bill across to him. "Keep the change."

The bartender nodded and moved on to the next customer.

Jaron sipped the drink and thought about his next move. He had driven all that way to deliver a message, and he'd do that with compassion and understanding, because at the end of the day Travis had still lost someone. That fact hadn't changed regardless that he was a cheating bastard who deserved a kick in the balls. He took a deep breath in and let it out slowly, counting to ten. Calm. Calm. He wouldn't kick anyone ever.

His eyes were gritty from lack of sleep, and his emotions threatened to spill over because of it. Adding alcohol to the mess wasn't his smartest move.

He pushed his half-full drink away and climbed off the stool, grabbing his bag from the floor.

Shoring up as much courage as he could muster, he crossed the room. He tapped Travis on the shoulder and swallowed down all the violent urges. Anger kept the hurt at bay. It wouldn't for long, though. He needed to be alone when he finally broke down.

Travis and the woman stopped swaying to the music before he turned. His eyes widened, and he smiled. "You're here."

Jaron nodded.

Travis took him in his arms and hugged him. Jaron let him but didn't return the hug, his body stiffening. His discomfort must have alerted Travis to the fact something was wrong. He pulled back but cupped Jaron's face. "What has that look on your face, baby?"

God, Jaron couldn't take it anymore. He stepped back. "Don't touch me. Don't you ever..." Jaron stopped, he took a couple of deep breaths to calm down, closing his eyes so he wouldn't have to see Travis.

"What the hell?" Travis' confusion had Jaron opening his eyes. Travis looked from the woman back to Jaron again. "No, baby. You got it wrong. Amber and I are—"

Jaron held up a hand. "I can't hear the excuses right now."

"I understand you're angry." The woman took a step in Jaron's direction.

"I'm beyond angry, but that isn't the point. It's also none of your business." Jaron met Travis' gaze.

Travis had a tic in his jaw, and his expression suggested he was about as angry as Jaron felt.

"Get her away from me. I mean it, Travis."

Amber rolled her eyes. "I'll go but know that you're gonna feel like shit once it's all straightened out."

She left him and Travis standing on the edge of the dance floor. She went to a booth in the corner and sat next to another woman, dressed in jeans and boots. Amber laid her head on the woman's shoulder and laced their fingers together. They seemed...together. Not just together but like *together*, together. Comfortable with each other enough to share living space and finances.

Jaron sighed and ran his hand down his face. He didn't have the energy to figure out what the hell that meant so he didn't try. He said the first thing that came to his mind. "Trick is gone. I truly am very sorry for your loss."

"I figured that's why you came." Travis looked as if Jaron had delivered a kick to the balls after all.

Jaron nodded and walked away, heading out of the bar. He stopped when Travis yelled across the room. "You're not even going to hear me out."

Jaron turned, meeting Travis' gaze. "I'm tired, Travis. Too tired for this right now." And he was five seconds from losing his shit. He didn't want to do that in front of Travis and the rest of the bar.

Travis closed the distance between them and took him by the elbow. He wanted to pull out of his hold, but his brain went fuzzy. "Have you slept at all?"

"No."

"You drove straight here?" Travis gave him the side-eye as he led him through the lobby to the front desk.

"Yes."

"Jesus, Jaron. No wonder." Travis sighed in frustration. "I guess you called it. Got what you wanted, didn't you?"

Jaron shook his head and fought the tears that swam in his eyes.

Travis stopped at the front desk. "Can I get an extra key to my room, please?"

The woman behind the front desk darted her gaze to Jaron before turning to Travis, smiling. "Certainly, sir."

Travis gave his name and room number. The woman handed him a card with the hotel's logo on the front. "Can I help you with anything else, sir?"

"No thanks." Travis took the card and headed to the elevator. Once they were inside, he handed the keycard to Jaron.

Jaron took it with shaky fingers.

"Have you eaten?"

"No."

Travis sighed again and looked straight ahead. Shiny metal reflected their blurry images standing next to each other. The door slid open and Travis guided Jaron down the hall to the left.

They stopped in front of a door about halfway down. Travis fished around in his pocket and pulled out his keycard before using it to open the door. He let Jaron go in first.

Jaron dropped his bag onto the floor beside the bed and sat down. He wanted to close his eyes, but if he did, he'd fall asleep, and they had a few things to talk about first. He opened his mouth to speak, but Travis held up his hand.

"Not right now. You're tired, and I'm pissed. We'll both say things we don't mean. Best if you take a shower. I'll bring you clean clothes."

Jaron nodded and stood, undressing before heading to the bathroom.

"What do you want to eat?" Travis asked from the other side of the door.

Jaron turned on the water for the shower, adjusting the spray.

The door opened, and Travis poked his head in. "What do you want to eat, baby?"

Jaron shrugged and didn't meet his gaze. Tears fell, and they came from a place of pure exhaustion.

"Pizza?"

Jaron shrugged again and stepped into the shower.

Travis sighed, and closed the door.

Travis had laid boxers and a T-shirt next to the sink for him. He must have gone through Jaron's bag, not that Jaron cared. He didn't have anything to hide. He dried off and got dressed before leaving the bathroom. A part of him had expected Travis to leave the room, but he sat with his back against the headboard of the bed. He had on pajama pants, and that was it. He flipped through the television channels.

"Pizza will be here in a few minutes." Travis never looked his way as he spoke.

The heater unit below the window churned out warm air.

Jaron stood there and let the last hour wash through his mind. Anger came back to him easily. "Don't you have a woman to go back to?"

Travis' gaze snapped to him. "Don't start with me, Jaron."

"I'm just wondering why you're still here."

"Besides the fact that it's my room."

Jaron narrowed his eyes. "Yeah, besides that."

"I love you. That's why I'm still here." Travis put the remote control on the side table beside the bed and stood. He pointed to it. "Lie down before you fall."

Jaron sighed and obeyed Travis. He climbed on the bed and lay down. "You're a shithead for saying that to me after that scene downstairs."

Travis sat on the bed beside him and picked up the remote again. "I'm not the shithead here, Jaron."

"Just go back to the bar and leave me alone."

"Go back to my cousin, you mean. I would, but she and her wife probably went back home by now."

Jaron sucked in a breath and burrowed into the covers. "Cousin?"

"Yeah. Kathleen and Amber own a horse farm just outside of town. She would have come to see me anyway, but she grew up riding Trick too. We were consoling each other."

Shit.

Travis turned to meet his gaze, giving Jaron a pointed stare.

Someone knocked, and that broke the spell. They both needed a reprieve anyway.

Travis got up and answered the door.

The smell of pizza hit him even before Travis paid the delivery guy.

He took a pizza in a box along with two bottles of water over to the table in the corner before waving Jaron over.

Jaron sat across from Travis and took a napkin. Travis opened the box, and the smell of pepperoni hit him. His stomach growled, and he took a piece. He moaned and shut his eyes when he took a bite. Jaron could feel Travis' gaze on him. When he opened them again, their gazes met and held. Neither spoke, but Jaron could see the hurt on Travis' face. He'd put that look there.

Jaron put the pizza on the napkin and hung his head. He took a deep breath before speaking "You don't deserve the lack of trust. You didn't earn it."

Travis nodded and took a bite of pizza. He chewed and swallowed before speaking. "Eat."

"I'm trying to apologize, Travis."

"I know. It can wait. Eat. Then Sleep. Tomorrow you'll go home, and I'll finish up with the buyer. We'll talk after I get home." Travis gestured to the pizza. "Eat."

"I don't want to go to bed with us fighting."

"Well, I'm not talking to you about this right now, Jaron. I'm not ready."

"Fine. But I want you to know that I love you too."

Travis' eyes had that sparkle they sometimes got, and he smiled. "That's the most important thing we needed to get settled."

Chapter
Twenty-Five

An ache had settled into Jaron's chest and made a home there. He didn't know if the cause had something to do with not settling things with Travis or if it had something to do with the separation from Bobby for two nights in a row.

Probably a combination of both.

He would have felt better if he could have made things right with Travis before he left for home, but he had a feeling Travis needed to roll their argument through his mind a few hundred more times.

Jaron sighed even as he pulled off the highway. As much as he wanted things to get back to normal, Travis didn't exactly give him a choice but to accept the timeline of fixing things. Maybe he didn't deserve one. Regardless, he owed Travis, so he'd let him have his way. The unsettled feeling wasn't comfortable, though, and probably wouldn't go away until they talked and made up.

Please, let us make up.

Jaron turned right off the exit. It was a straight shot into Pickleville, but he had to drive through Harbor Shire to get there.

Jaron hadn't been away from Bobby for more than one night since Tracy had given birth. The separation felt foreign, as if an alien lived inside him, churning things up.

Not long before he got to see Bobby again. The anticipation built until his hands shook. He smiled at just the thought of getting to hug his son.

He barely remembered what his life had been like before Bobby came. Fatherhood had stuck to him, not letting go. He worried about messing up all the time and wondered how his decisions would affect Bobby. Everything he did, he thought of Bobby first. It had been rooted in his brain since day one. Maybe even before that.

Travis had said he'd make Bobby a part of his family for the rest of his life and Jaron had believed him. Why hadn't Jaron believed Travis when it came to himself? He hadn't, though. And didn't until last night's fiasco. It wasn't even about what Travis had said but the fact that he took care of Jaron even though the scene in the bar had pissed him off.

Jaron had wanted to paint Travis as the partier he had been in high school. Knowing that Travis would flit around from one person's bed to the next would protect Jaron's heart. But the truth was he'd never known the kind of person Travis was even back in high school. If he had, he would have seen that Travis was loyal to his friends, counting them as family and sticking by them regardless of when they fucked up.

He had believed rumors from people who only ever wanted to hear themselves speak. They didn't care about the words that came out of their mouths.

His cell phone rang, startling him out of his musings, and he jumped. He pulled over onto the side of the road before picking up the phone off the passenger's seat.

When he saw Travis' number, his heart picked up a bit. He took a deep breath and answered. "Hi."

"Hey. Just wanted to tell you I'm gonna be an extra day."

Jaron opened his mouth to speak and then closed it again. He wanted to ask why and if Travis stayed away an extra day because he needed more time to think. And if he did, did that mean he contemplated ending things? All he said was, "Oh. Okay."

"My buyer told me about a cattlewoman who has a special breeding program I'm thinking about trying. She's further south. It will take me an extra day. Should be home by the afternoon tomorrow."

"Your other meeting went okay?" Jaron wanted to ask if they were okay. The uncertainty twisted his gut.

"Better than. I think the guy will buy from us in the future. Especially if I decide to get this new breed."

"Are they beef cows?"

"Yeah, but I'd be starting a breeding program. Mixing them with the Angus I already have. A few others have done that, and the result was smaller cattle, so they're easier to keep, but they have the meat quality of the Angus." The excitement came through clear as day even through the phone.

"It sounds complicated."

Travis made a noncommittal sound in the back of his throat. "Are you home yet?"

"Almost. Just on the outside of Harbor Shire." Jaron thought about what he should say next, forming the words in his mind. "Travis, I—"

"I gotta go. I'll call you tonight."

"Okay. I love you."

"I love you too, baby." Travis' tone more than his words eased that place in Jaron that feared he might have fucked things up beyond repair. Maybe they still had a lot to figure out about each other, but that wasn't a bad thing necessarily.

When they hung up, Jaron smiled. They hadn't fixed everything yet, but at least he knew the problem wasn't a deal breaker. He pulled the car back onto the road.

He made his way through Harbor Shire with little issue, getting caught up at two lights and having to wait. The town wasn't big, but it wasn't as small as Pickleville. The Harbor had a few supermarket chain stores and some fast food restaurants along the main drag.

When the stores turned into houses that spread out farther from each other and changed into fields Jaron's mind went back to Travis again.

He needed to make a gesture. Something big so that Travis knew his intentions. But what?

Jaron went straight to the main house. His mother had called before he'd left the hotel and told him she'd dropped Bobby off with Beverly. She said something about Bobby helping Greg feed the horses.

He parked next to the other farm vehicles and shut off the engine. Bobby and Greg walked out of the horse barn together. Greg smiled at something Bobby said and ruffled his hair. He pointed at Jaron.

Bobby stopped and looked his way before running over.

As soon as Jaron held Bobby, his world became right. The ache in his chest lessened, and he could breathe again. "I missed you so, so much."

Bobby hugged Jaron back. "Missed you too. But guess what? I got to give hay to all the horses. I gave them water too but Greg had to carry the bucket. And Grandma Bev told me she had ice cream for when we're done."

Jaron chuckled. "Ice cream, huh?"

"Yep." Bobby took Jaron's hand and led him into the house.

Greg followed close behind them.

"Thanks for letting Bobby help with the horses."

"Did a good job. Wanna help every day after school?"

"Okay."

Home felt good.

Chapter Twenty-Six

♥

J aron walked out of the main house and down to the end of the driveway. He had his cell phone in his pocket, and he wasn't sure why. Normally he never carried it, but he put it into his pocket that morning and hadn't taken it out even when he began cleaning the main house.

He felt off kilter. The phone grounded him in a way he couldn't totally explain. Maybe because it was the only way he could get in touch with Travis. He'd never been a needy person, so he didn't think that was it.

Whatever. It was just a phone in his pocket. A little thing that made him feel a bit safer.

The field across the road had cows in it. A black and white cow locked her gaze with his and slowly walked over. The rest of the herd didn't give him a passing glance.

The grass came up to the top of her hooves. The herd hadn't made it as far over as the fence yet.

"Don't you have pretty eyes." Jaron smiled and looked at his watch.

Bobby's bus driver wouldn't like it if she had to worry about him crossing the road in front of the bus. She always had a smile for Bobby when he got on the bus and when he got off. She had a treat for the kids who rode her bus every Friday. Most of the time it was a small piece of candy, but Bobby loved getting them. She didn't seem to like adults, though. Or maybe it was Jaron.

Jaron had time, so he crossed the road. The cow took a step back, eying him with suspicion. He held out his hand. "It's all right. I won't hurt you." He kept his voice at no more than a whisper.

She blew through her nose and stomped a hoof. Her eyes went wild with suspicion. She proved brave enough to take a step in his direction, though. Her nose almost touched his hand when the purr of a vehicle engine and the steady rotation of rubber on gravel sounded off to Jaron's left. The cow stiffened, and she moved away. Her friends stopped grazing when the sound of tires rolled to a stop.

It was only then that Jaron looked up.

Brad sat behind the wheel of a small red truck. His blond hair was covered with a baseball cap. Their gazes met, and Jaron could see the glassiness of his eyes. Alcohol had flushed Brad's cheeks.

The driver's side door opened, and Brad got out.

Jaron sucked in a breath and froze when he saw the aluminum bat in Brad's hand. Every sound disappeared except for his own breath.

Brad's lips moved and then curled in disgust.

Jaron shook his head, not understanding what Brad said.

Everything slowed, including his own breathing. His mind turned off, and instinct took over.

Jaron crossed the road as quickly as he could, but Brad closed the distance when he made it to the driveway.

Brad never said a word as he swung the bat. Jaron lifted his arm, wanting to protect his head. The impact drove his arm into his face, and he stumbled, falling to the ground.

Another hit landed across his hip. He held up his hands.

Brad had the bat raised. He had a blank look in his eyes as if his mind had gone somewhere else.

"M-my son. His bus is coming. Please."

Brad shook his head and blinked as if coming back from a foggy mind. He took a step back.

A gunshot vibrated through the air, startling them both. Brad jumped and hunched his shoulders, getting lower to the ground, when another gunshot cracked. Brad turned back to his truck as Greg ran over, a shotgun in his hand. He pointed it at Brad even after he took off down the road.

Greg put the gun down next to Jaron and knelt. "Where did he hit you?"

Jaron shut his eyes when Greg became blurry. His heartbeat pounded through his brain and he couldn't get enough oxygen into his lungs.

Greg cursed. "You're okay. He left, and Beverly is calling the police. But you need to calm down or you'll go into shock."

His vision went black, but he heard Greg speak.

"I've gotcha. No worries now."

Jaron heard the school bus pop and wheeze. And then he felt nothing. Someone held the hand of his good arm, and he could hear Bobby crying.

Beverly had a phone up to her ear. "An ambulance is on the way...Bobby's fine. He was still on the bus when Brad came...We're all very worried...Greg's making sure Brad doesn't come back. Jaron's well protected."

Jaron turned toward Bobby's soft sobs and opened his eyes. Beverly held his hand with Bobby tucked up next to her. Bobby touched his shoulder. Bobby's backpack lay on the grass a few feet away, forgotten. "Papa's here, baby."

"You didn't wake up." Bobby wiggled around and laid his head on Jaron's shoulder.

"Careful." Beverly had a hand on Bobby's arm but let him go when Jaron nodded. "He's awake...okay." She fiddled with the phone and then held it out.

"I'm on my way." Everyone heard Travis over the speakerphone. "Hang in there."

"I will."

"I'll meet you at the hospital."

"Papa's gotta go to the hospital?" Bobby didn't move from beside Jaron.

"He sure does, but the doctors are gonna make him feel better." Travis was the one who answered.

"He's not gonna never wake up like Mommy?"

Jaron shut his eyes when Bobby asked that question.

Travis made a sound through the phone that Jaron couldn't identify until he heard the shakiness in his voice. "I'll make him wake up."

"You're gonna take care of Papa?"

"Yeah. And you. I'll see you in less than one hour."

Bobby nodded and stuck his thumb in his mouth.

Jaron tried to breathe through the pain. The sirens, growing closer, eased some of his tension, and he closed his eyes again.

Beverly squeezed his hand. "Don't go to sleep, Jaron."

Bobby lifted his head. "You're gonna wake up?" Jaron could hear the tears in every word.

He tightened his hold on Bobby. "Yeah, snuggle bear. Papa's leg hurts, is all." He was pretty sure he had a broken arm as well and he had a headache.

Travis cursed. "I'll be there as soon as I can, baby."

The sirens grew so close he couldn't hear anything except their loud, shrill calls. The next thing he knew paramedics knelt beside him. When they tried to separate Bobby from Jaron, Bobby threw a fit.

He kicked and called for Jaron when Beverly tried pulling him away.

"Take me off speaker and let me talk to Bobby, Mom." Something in Travis' tone calmed Jaron even if it didn't do anything for Bobby.

Whatever conversation Travis had with Bobby gained his full attention.

Jaron noticed a police officer talking to Greg.

Greg had the shotgun in his arms, held to the side toward the field.

The officer didn't take it away from him, which meant the cop knew Greg wasn't a threat. The officer probably knew Greg, if not personally then he certainly knew Greg's family.

One of the paramedics smiled at him. A woman in a police uniform stood directly behind the paramedic. "Want to tell me what happened?"

Jaron's head ached, but he still wanted to answer. "Um...I was waiting for Bobby's bus. I went to pet the cow across the road when Brad Flynn stopped on the road. He was drunk. Had a bat. He hit me twice."

The paramedic asked the next question. "Did he get you in the head?"

"I put my arm up when he swung. He hit it, and my arm hit my head."

The paramedic smiled. "You'll be okay."

Jaron nodded and shut his eyes as they worked on him.

Chapter
Twenty-Seven

♥

Travis expected the tension would lessen when he pulled into the hospital's parking lot, but it stayed in his chest, pushing against his sanity, threatening to send him into a million pieces. Jaron and Bobby needed him to stay together.

He was out of his truck and at the emergency rooms entrance within seconds. A woman stood behind a counter messing with a file full of papers. "Jaron McAllister."

"Are you family?"

"I-I'm his partner. Husband." If Travis had his way, he'd have that title sooner rather than later, but that wasn't why he lied. They wouldn't let him inside Jaron's room otherwise.

She nodded and typed on her computer before coming around the counter. "Follow me."

"How's he doing?"

"He's currently in X-ray. Once he gets done there, you'll get a chance to see him."

"Thanks."

She led him to a waiting area.

Gloria and his mom sat next to each other. They both had the same worried expression on their faces. His mom gave him a relieved smile the second he stepped into the large room.

The nurse who had led him back disappeared.

Bobby sat on Gloria's lap but scrambled off as soon as he saw Travis. Travis knelt and opened his arms, scooping Bobby up the second he had his little body in his arms. Bobby wrapped his arms around Travis' neck, sniffling. "They took Papa."

"They have to do tests."

"Make them bring him back."

Travis rubbed circles across Bobby's back. "The nurse said we can have him back when they finish doing tests."

Bobby tried to shake his head, but the movement was awkward with his face pressed into Travis' neck.

"What if we hang together?"

Bobby lifted his head and moved so he could meet Travis' gaze. "You won't leave me?"

"Not ever."

"Like Papa doesn't. 'cept when he's sick."

"He's not going to leave you, little man. The doctors need to make him feel better. That's all."

"And then I can have him back?"

"Yeah." Travis smiled, trying not to let the worry show. It hadn't lessened even inside the hospital. "Then we can have him back. We'll have to take care of him."

Bobby nodded. "We'll make him all better, huh?"

"We sure will."

Bobby lay his head on Travis's shoulder and sighed. "I still want Papa."

"Me too, little man. Me too." Travis walked across the room and sat next to his mom. He had to adjust Bobby on his lap before he settled.

When his mother spoke, it was in low whispers. "Jaron went out to wait for Bobby's bus. Next thing I know, Greg storms in the house asking for a gun. If it weren't for him, it would have been a lot worse."

"Did the cops get Brad?"

"The police chief came by about ten minutes ago and told us Brad turned himself in."

He knew the chief. He'd been in enough trouble during his high school years to annoy the poor guy. He had even taken Travis home a time or two. All of his troublemaking included Jackson and Brad. The chief would let Travis talk to Brad because he knew the three of them did bad shit together. Talking wasn't what Travis had in mind, though.

Travis pulled his phone out of his pocket with his free hand and flipped it open. He was about to use his thumb to text Jackson to meet him at the police station, but Bobby shifted on his lap. Travis gazed down at those big blue eyes staring at the phone screen. Bobby couldn't read. He knew that, but it didn't matter.

Instead, he looked around his mother to Gloria. "Is there anyone Jaron would want us to call?"

"I've called Brian and his friend from the city. Both are on their way." Gloria gave him a smile that didn't quite meet her eyes.

Travis nodded and dialed Jackson's number with his thumb. It took Jackson one ring to answer. "I just heard. I hope to fuck you're in town."

"Just got here."

"Don't do anything stupid. You have the kid to think of." Jackson knew him well.

"I know."

"Good. I'm on my way."

Bobby climbed from Travis' lap and stared at him for long seconds.

"Hold on, Jackson." He moved the phone away from his ear and held it out to Bobby. "You want to talk to him?"

Bobby nodded and took it, putting it up to his ear. "My Papa got hurt. Travis said the doctors are fixing him." Whatever Jackson said made Bobby nod. "Yeah. He slept on the ground and wouldn't wake up. But now he's awake."

God, Bobby would talk about it for a while, even after everything settled down. The poor kid had been traumatized twice in the span of months.

Travis ran a hand down his face. How the hell did he let Brad happen? And for a second time. If he had been there, he could have stopped it. Instead, he used some stupid cows to avoid Jaron for an extra day. His feelings getting hurt didn't seem all that important in the face of Jaron's injuries.

His mother leaned over. "There's one person to blame, and he's in a jail cell." Leave it to his mother to read his mind.

Travis nodded and ran a hand down Bobby's arm even as he chatted Jackson up on the phone.

He didn't get a chance to reply before someone in scrubs came into the room. "Gloria McAllister?"

Gloria stood. The woman in scrubs walked over to them.

Travis sat straighter, wrapping his arm around Bobby's waist.

"He broke his arm and has a concussion. His arm stopped him from sustaining a worse head injury." She pursed her lips and sighed. "We're not sure about the damage to his leg yet. We're still assessing the injury. When I get the tests back, I'll let you know." She turned her gaze to Travis. "You must be Travis. He's asking for you. If you'd follow me."

Travis didn't ask if he could take Bobby with him. Where Travis went, Bobby went, especially if they got to see Jaron.

He lifted Bobby in his arms and followed her out of the waiting room.

"We get to see Papa. I gotta go." Bobby handed the phone to Travis.

Travis didn't bother checking if Jackson was on the other end of the phone. He closed the screen and stuck it into his pocket.

Bobby wiggled and vibrated with energy.

The lady in scrubs pressed a button on the wall, and a giant door opened. They walked through together and came to a room with a curtain pulled closed. The number twenty-two stuck on the wall next to the room. She smiled and gestured.

Travis nodded and pushed the curtain out of the way with his free hand. Jaron lay on one of those smaller emergency room cot things with his arm in a sling and temporary cast-type contraption. His eyes were closed, but they opened when Bobby made a sobbing sound. Jaron looked small and pasty white. Around his eyes held the only color but they bruised with tiredness.

Jaron lit up a bit when he saw them, smiling.

"Papa." Bobby just about jumped out of Travis' arms to get to Jaron.

"My left side." Jaron's voice sounded as if he'd gargled with gravel.

"He won't hurt you?" Travis held on to Bobby with both hands, trying to contain him until Jaron answered.

Jaron shook his head. "Not that side. Brad liked the right side. Besides, they have me on the good stuff."

That tension spiked a bit more. He tried to contain it, but the tension stiffened every muscle in his body.

"Sorry."

Travis laid Bobby down beside Jaron as gently as he could. "You don't have to apologize for him, baby."

"Not for him. For making a joke of it when you're not ready." Jaron wrapped an arm around Bobby and kissed the top of his head.

Bobby wrapped his arm around Jaron.

Travis leaned over and kissed Jaron. "I'm sorry."

"If I don't get to apologize, then you don't either."

Travis smiled and placed his hand on top of Jaron's. "I suppose that's fair." Travis pulled over one of the chairs and sat down again. "Do you need anything?"

Jaron shook his head. "Just you and Bobby."

Travis took his hand in both of his. "You got us, baby."

An older woman in blue scrubs came in. She had short blonde hair and a tan. She smiled at Jaron. "You're a lucky man, Mr. McAllister. Your hip will heal with rest and a little ice. I'll subscribe something for the swelling and pain."

"No lasting damage?"

"Not to his hip. We'll need to set his arm. He lost consciousness. Whether from the pain or the head injury is unclear. That's the main concern at the moment. He'll have to follow-up with his family physician."

Travis already had a to-do list running in his mind and put making an appointment for Jaron at the top of the list.

"So can I go home?"

She shook her head. "You'll be here at least overnight for observation because of the head injury."

Travis hoped the hospital had cots big enough for a grown man and a six-year-old boy because he wasn't leaving Jaron.

By the time they moved Jaron to a normal room, more people had arrived. Jackson, Brian, Greg, and one guy Travis had never met packed into Jaron's small hospital room.

Bobby sat on Travis' lap, and they played *I Spy* while Jaron slept.

His mother and Gloria sat on chairs talking quietly to each other while Greg kept sneaking quick glances at Brian.

Brian didn't seem to notice even though they stood next to each other.

The Latino man who stood by Jaron's bedside and held the hand on his good arm never missed a thing, including Greg's crush on Brian.

Travis sat in a chair to the left of Jaron's bed in the back of the room with the stranger on the other side, facing Travis and Bobby.

Jackson sat next to Travis and ignored everyone.

Travis knew what Brad did would bother Jackson on a whole different level than it did him.

Jackson had a soft spot for the wounded. It was why he sat in Jaron's hospital room and it was also why he wanted to find a way to help Brad.

They both knew what kind of home Brad came from and it wasn't a pretty environment. Travis had seen Brad's dad so drunk he'd fallen over and he'd seen him try to pick a fight with his children more than once. He couldn't bring himself to give a crap. Not when Jaron lay in a bed half broken. Just picturing Brad taking a bat...yeah, the thought turned his stomach.

"I spy something blue."

Bobby looked around the room at first, but his gaze landed on the stranger. The stranger darted his gaze to the dry erase marker on a board opposite Jaron's hospital bed. Bobby giggled and said, "The marker."

Travis tickled Bobby. "Cheater."

Bobby giggled even more and wiggled around on his lap. "It's helping, not cheating."

"Cheating." Travis tickled Bobby's belly a couple of more times before giving Bobby a break.

Travis met the stranger's gaze. "I'm Travis. Jaron's boyfriend."

"Andrew Martinez. Jaron's best friend." Andrew spoke with a slight accent and had a way of assessing the entire room, seeing every small detail in a matter of seconds. "Jaron talked about you."

Travis smiled. "He did you too. It's nice meeting you finally."

"Will I have to stay to keep Jaron safe? Because I will and can."

Travis winced and shook his head. "No, sir."

Andrew nodded once, but his focus changed when Jaron turned his head. "Hey, there you are, vato."

Jaron smiled. "You came."

"Of course." Andrew leaned down. "Maybe small town isn't for you."

Jaron smiled. His eyes were half-closed.

The tension in his face told Travis he was in pain, but Travis let Jaron have his moment with Andrew for a little bit longer. He thought Jaron needed that more than he needed pain medication.

"I promise. It is," Jaron whispered. His voice was husky.

"You say the word, and I'll arrest every homophobic prick here." Andrew's jaw muscles ticced.

"Can't arrest everyone," Jaron said.

"No, but we can kick some serious..." Travis was the one who spoke but stopped when he got to the word *ass*, not wanting Bobby to hear it.

Jaron turned his head until he met Travis' gaze. "No."

Travis sighed and let the tension swallow him again. "I'm just saying sending a message might be a good idea."

Brian cleared his throat. "I don't know. Seems to me we're starting to outnumber the homophobes in Pickleville now. And those guys aren't worth the effort anyway."

"Three of us isn't exactly a high number," Travis protested.

"Papa, what's a homophobe?" Bobby played with Travis' fingers.

"Someone who doesn't like me because I like boys instead of girls."

Bobby's brow wrinkled. "Oh. No one will like me if I like boys?"

"Just some people, little man. And those people aren't your friends anyway," Travis answered because he could see Jaron fading fast. And him getting upset at Travis' outburst certainly didn't help his healing efforts.

Bobby turned to Jackson. "You like boys?" Why Bobby targeted Jackson with that question, Travis had no idea, but whatever.

"I like everybody. Girls and boys." Jackson smiled and turned to Brian, winking in a flirting way. "Guess that makes four."

Greg narrowed his eyes at Jackson and shook his head. "Five. And Leonard makes six. Neil makes seven. And my friend Kyler makes eight." Greg's expression softened when he looked at Brian. "So you're right."

"Thank you, Greg. And Brian. And Jackson." Jaron smiled at each one of them before turning his gaze to Travis, giving him a pointed stare Travis thought Jaron only reserved for Bobby. Even tired, Jaron's silent reprimand came through loud and clear. "So, no fighting. Promise me."

Travis knew if he didn't promise it would stress Jaron out, which was the last thing his love needed. "I promise, baby." Travis gave Jaron a pointed look of his own. "Now press the button on the pain thing and get some rest."

Travis elbowed Jackson in the side. Jackson startled before standing. "Right. Time to go, everyone. Travis will keep us posted. We'll all descend on Jaron when he's home."

Andrew squeezed Jaron's hand before stepping away. "Which one of you is gonna show me around town?"

Greg shrugged. "Sure. No problem."

Andrew put an arm around Greg's shoulder and led him out of the room. "You're the one who scared Flynn away, right?"

Greg nodded.

"Nice job. Didn't hurt anyone but still defused the situation."

Travis smiled and thought maybe he liked Andrew.

Brian leaned down and kissed Jaron on the cheek. "I'm glad you're okay, Jaron."

"Thanks for coming."

"Always." Brian waved at Travis and then at Bobby.

Beverly and Gloria were the last to leave, and Gloria hovered for long minutes, her hands shaking as she moved Jaron's hair off his forehead. She didn't say anything, but then she didn't have to. Jaron was her baby, and he got hurt. Mama Bear wanted to protect, and if she left, she couldn't do that. She gave Travis a look that said he'd better take care of Jaron.

Travis nodded and hugged Bobby closer. "I got this."

Gloria turned and left the room.

Travis stood and pulled the chair closer to Jaron. He turned to Bobby. "Your turn to spy, little man."

Bobby leaned against him and put his thumb in his mouth. "Maybe we can watch TV."

Jaron watched them with a smile.

Travis winked and reached over for the tan box thing that would turn on the television and call the nurse all at the same time. The television hung on the wall opposite the end of the bed. Even when it turned on, Jaron never averted his gaze.

Travis met his gaze again and smiled. "What's wrong, baby? Do you need anything? Water? The bathroom?"

Jaron shook his head. "Move back in. With Bobby and me. Like a real family. Together."

"Why don't we talk about this when we get home?"

"No, Travis. I'm ready now."

"Okay but I have a lot of clothes. You sure we'll have enough closet space." Travis might have made a joke of it but inside all the pieces aligned.

Chapter
Twenty-Eight

♥

The second Jaron stepped outside onto the porch, Travis and Jackson stopped talking.

Like that's not obvious at all. Jaron rolled his eyes.

Jackson had stayed since Jaron had gotten out of the hospital. He slept on the couch while Andrew took the guest room.

Jaron got the impression the incident with Brad bothered him to the point he needed the solidarity of the only other friend in their little trio that he had left. In high school, the three of them were always together. Brad had broken the friendship. Not so much by hurting Jaron. Well, also that. But Jaron thought Brad beating him represented the lack of acceptance. It might have been okay as long as one of them didn't start a long-term relationship. They could all sit at the bar and pretend. The illusion had gone up in smoke the second Travis had started something serious with Jaron. Jackson was the glue that held the friendship together in some respects, and maybe he felt as if he'd failed.

He hobbled over to Travis and sat on his lap.

Travis put his arms around him and held him, careful to avoid his injured hip.

The thing still hurt enough that he limped a bit, and it restricted his movements, which annoyed him more than anything else. He wanted to get back to work but that wasn't possible, not just because of his hip but his arm had weeks left to go before the cast was off. He had to face Jackson when he sat because the other side would hurt his hip.

He gave Travis a look he hoped conveyed he wasn't a big fan of secrets. "You two are talking about Brad. I already know you are."

Jackson smiled and answered. The smile didn't quite reach his eyes. "He pled guilty. He's getting a few years in prison."

"But?" There was a *but* coming. Jaron could tell. Jaron had an urge to run as fast as his gimpy ass could to the main barn where Bobby helped Greg feed the horses and protect him. It didn't matter that Andrew was with them or that Greg could hold his own when it came down to it.

"But Brad has two brothers who need him."

Jaron sighed in relief and put his cast-covered hand to his chest. "I thought you were gonna tell me he escaped or something."

"Brad knows he fucked up. He'll take his punishment." Travis' jaw muscles ticced. "He's always been good about that."

Jackson nodded. "Luis can probably financially support himself and Cadon. He works a steady job. He's still young, though. Nineteen. Cadon is what...eleven."

"Well, Brad's actions certainly don't reflect on them. Or shouldn't." Jaron thought about the gossip he always heard at the grocery store. Some people were vicious. "Yeah, I see the problem."

"It's already started. I heard Cadon got into a fight at school and got suspended. He's home alone because Luis can't afford to take off work."

Jaron stood slowly and held out his hand to Travis. "Can I borrow your truck?"

"No." Travis softened the blow with a smile. "But I'll drive you."

Jaron hobbled his way down the stairs and over to Travis' truck. "Are you guys coming?"

Travis and Jackson both stood at the same time. Travis helped Jaron into the passenger's seat.

Jackson climbed into the back seat before Travis made it around to the driver's side. "Thank you for doing this."

"It's not their fault. And it has to be me who makes friends, don't you think?"

Jackson nodded and patted Jaron on the shoulder. "I think people will back off sooner, yeah."

A comfortable silence fell between them on the way to town.

When Travis pulled in front of a mechanics garage, he put the truck in park but didn't shut off the engine before he got out and made his way around the front of the truck to Jaron. Travis helped him out and stole a kiss before he let Jaron go.

"You want me to go with you?"

Jaron noticed one of the cops watching them from across the street. Most of the cops parked in the lot there. The police station was a couple of buildings over. His stares just proved one thing. "I should go by myself."

Travis nodded and shut the passenger's side door. He didn't bother sitting back in the truck but leaned against it, watching Jaron walk to the front door that said they were open.

A bigger guy with a scowl sat behind a desk. A boxy computer sat to the left and paperwork on the upper right corner. That was Royce, who'd bought up several businesses in town and made it a safer place to live.

The guy gave Jaron the once over and didn't say a word.

"I'm Jaron McAllister. I'd like to talk to Luis Flynn."

"Not gonna happen if you're here to start shit with him."

Jaron shook his head. "No, sir. The exact opposite in fact."

"Fine." The guy walked over to a large window that separated the small office from the rest of the garage. He knocked on it and crooked a finger at someone.

Jaron assumed he made the gesture at Luis.

"Now." Royce seemed like a hard ass. Jaron could see why the homophobes in Pickleville didn't mess with him. It wasn't just because he bought up several businesses.

A few seconds later and a guy with long dark-blond hair stood there with some type of wrench in his hand. The guy looked enough like Brad that Jaron saw the family resemblance right off. Brad had a square jawline and prominent features. Luis had more of a delicate bone structure. "I was right in the middle...oh." His gaze met Jaron's, and his face turned bright red.

Jaron smiled and took a step in his direction with his good arm out. Luis hesitated, but he shook Jaron's hand. "I'm Jaron. I know you don't know me. And I know this is going to sound very forward, but would it be all right if Cadon stayed over on the farm with us while you're at work? Jackson and Travis told me about his suspension. They can give him riding lessons or whatever if he wants."

The surprise clearly showed on Luis' face. "You want to babysit my little brother?"

"Well, yeah, I guess." Jaron shrugged. "I mean I know school is already out for today. And Bobby would love having another kid around. Greg might technically be an adult but he's got a lot of kid left in him. And he's way too serious all the time. It would do him good to have another kid around besides Bobby."

"You're serious?"

Jaron gestured to the door behind him. "Travis and Jackson are outside in the truck. You should talk to them. You know, since you know them. You definitely shouldn't let a stranger take your little brother anywhere." Jaron smiled and nodded, turning a bit to give him room to pass.

Luis gave him an open-mouthed stare but moved past him and out of the door. He held it open for Jaron and waited for him to limp through. The injury ached a bit from him standing on it too long.

Luis must have noticed him wincing. "Are you okay?"

Jaron waved off the concern. "I'm fine. Honestly."

Travis closed the distance between them and wrapped an arm around Jaron's waist. He led Jaron to the passenger's seat and lifted him up before Jaron had a chance to protest. Jackson got out, and all three men stood in the open doorway.

"You guys want to help us after what Brad did?" Luis kept his head down and both hands wrapped around the wrench as if it were the only thing that grounded him.

Travis sighed. "Not your fault. Or Cadon's."

Luis looked up. "Not everyone thinks that."

"We know. That's why we're here." Travis' jaw muscles jumped. "Look, I might want to kick Brad's ass right now, but that doesn't have anything to do with you and Cadon. We're not gonna let people think otherwise. So if you let us, we'll get Cadon and bring him to the farm. Maybe you can pick him up later and stay for dinner."

Luis nodded. "I-I guess that would be okay."

Travis pulled Luis into a hug. Travis ended the hug but guided him over to Jaron. Jaron leaned down and hugged Luis. "We're here to help."

"Thank you." Luis' voice shook when he spoke, and he hugged Jaron just a little tighter, as if he needed some strength. When he pulled away, he seemed relieved. "Seriously. Thank you."

"I know what it's like living with an addict. Makes you feel helpless. Doesn't matter how much you talk to them. And I know how much you love him anyway. And I know what it's like raising a kid through all that." Jaron tried not to let the emotion well up in his chest but failed. "You're not alone."

Luis initiated the hug the second time around, and when he let go, he smiled for the first time. "Can I bring anything to dinner?"

"Just yourself." Jaron couldn't help but feel as if he had made a new friend. And out of such an ugly, violent scene.

Luis' boss stood in the open doorway of the office with that same scowl on his face. He crooked a finger at Luis, who sighed. "I gotta go. See you guys later."

Jaron watched as Luis jogged back to the garage.

"Are you appreciating his ass?" Travis looked from Jaron to Luis and back again.

"No. The fact that he can jog. I miss moving at a fast pace." Jaron really did.

Jackson snorted out a laugh and got back into the truck.

Travis moved into the open space, crowding Jaron, cupping his cheek. That sparkle of mischief made a home in his eyes. "How about I show you a fast pace later tonight?"

Jaron grinned. "None of that gentle stuff you've been giving me."

"I'll pound you good, baby."

Jaron chuckled. "You know just what to say to charm a guy."

****

Unrequited love sucks. Especially for Greg Mitchell, who has to watch the man of his dreams date every guy in town except for him.

Don't want to leave Pickleville? Stay in town by getting your copy of here. Or scan the QR Code.

****

All battles leave scars. Some are different than others. **Redefining Normal** is yours FREE when you sign up for my Newsletter. Or scan the QR code.

****

Honest reviews of my books help bring them to the attention of other readers. Leaving a review will help readers find the book. You can leave a review here: https://www.amazon.com/review/create-review/B01N5QOER2

About the Author

♥

April Kelley is an author of LGBT Romance. Her works include *The Journey of Jimini Renn*, which was a Rainbow Awards finalist, the *Saint Lakes* series, and over thirty more.

Living in Southwest Michigan, April resides with her husband and two kids. She has been an avid reader for several years. Ever since she wrote her first story at the age of ten, the characters in her head still won't stop telling their stories. If April isn't reading or writing, she can be found outside playing with the animals or taking a long walk in the woods.

If you wish to contact her, email authoraprilkelley@gmail.com.

Please visit her website at https://authoraprilkelley.com/

Printed in Great Britain
by Amazon